THE RIFT OF SHADOWS

Damian Blackwood

contents

Prologue

In the distant future, the streets of Chicago would stand as a busy metropolis. People of all ages, races, and backgrounds filled this city and made it the fine place that it was: diverse, fast-paced, and hectic. But like any city, of course, it had its problems: crime, drugs, and gangs. Chicago had seen its fair share of corruption, greed, and power shifts. To those people who inhabited the city, however, they called home. Chicagoans felt a profound sense of peace and security, and nothing could make them feel any different. They knew how to survive, how to weather the storm. That was until one fateful day changed everything that they knew and the worst storm they had ever known blew in...

A strange light emitted in the middle of the intersection at Taylor St. and Halsted St. directly next to the UIC campus. The winds had begun to pick up as the students and faculty all gathered on a nearby rooftop. Others had started to walk out in front of the building pulling out cell phones to get footage of the phenomenon.

"What is that?!" the people inquired.

No one knew the answer to that question. Many knew that they shouldn't have been in the area. However, a vast majority stood there waiting in anticipation of what events would follow.

The light grew brighter and stronger as time went on and became more unbearable as it started to pulse. At first, it was slow, rhythmic, and almost hypnotizing. For a moment, all was silent. Crowds began to gather around it as cars along the road stopped and the passengers got out to see the event. The curiosity of it all took away all sense of reasonableness.

Several people all went towards the strange light to get a closer look. As they made their way over, a strong energy field coming from the pulse sent the cars surrounding the area flying away from it. The people that gathered around the field disintegrated in an instant from the intense heat coming from it. Countless people lost their lives in less than five seconds.

Minutes later, the Chicago Police Department arrived at the scene with multiple SWAT teams to assess the threat. The priority was crowd control. Right away, they ordered all pedestrians and onlookers into the nearest building on campus to preserve some type of order. Many of the crowd still ignored the police order and the officers grew impatient with them. So, they used the K-9 unit, tear gas, and riot shields to drive them back.

Once the onlookers were inside and locked down, CPD then turned their attention to the more immediate issue – the strange light in the middle of the road. Because of the intensity of the light and what it did to the surrounding crowd, SWAT members did what they could to protect themselves. Equipped with bomb suits, officers began to move in slowly. The closer they got in, the stronger it became. Once they were a few feet out, the light expanded and, in an instant, they were all vaporized. In an instant, it was clear that the police were powerless to do anything. Immediately, the National Guard was called in.

The troops arrived on the scene thirty minutes later led by Major James Collins. With him, came over one hundred soldiers, all ready and waiting. Once they got in place, Collins gave the order for a cordon to be placed around the light and the Guard.

"Colonel Locke, the troops are in place," said Major Collins over the radio. "How should we proceed?"

"Use extreme caution, Major. We don't know what it is we're dealing with."

"Copy." Collins signaled Lieutenant Smith, the science officer, to come to him.

Collins was a decorated soldier with tenures in both the Army and the National Guard. He was a career soldier well on his way through the ranks who traveled the world and fought for his country to keep the peace. This, however, proved to be the greatest challenge to peace that he would ever face in his life.

"Lieutenant, what do you make of this?"

"Sir, it's unlike anything this world has ever seen. It has an energy field but there's no radiation coming from it."

"So, we're not in any immediate danger?"

"I wouldn't say that, sir."

"Explain."

"Sir, what I'm thinking doesn't fall in line with anything that any type of known science can explain. The truth is, we don't know what this is," Smith said hesitantly.

But Collins insisted, "Humor me, Lieutenant. I need some sort of idea of what we're dealing with here."

"A doorway, Major," Smith said. "What if it's a doorway?"

Collins appeared puzzled at the prospect of what he was saying. "A doorway to what, Lieutenant?"

"Who knows? It could be a doorway to another planet, another realm, or simply another part of the world. Honestly, the possibilities are endless. I'm afraid we're in uncharted territory here, sir."

"You're talking science fiction movies here, son," Collins insisted. "Nothing like that exists nor can exist."

But Smith persisted, "Sir, what's happening right now in front of us doesn't line up with anything reality has ever shown us and, therefore, shouldn't exist. But it's right here in front of us. That alone is another reason that we need to just throw out everything that we know." Smith, then hesitantly said, "I think we seriously need to consider the possibility of an invasion of some kind."

Collins took a moment to think the situation through. "Could that be what's happening?" he thought to himself. However, that time was cut short as the energy field began to pulse again, only this time, much stronger and far brighter than before.

Collins commanded, "Alright, soldiers. Arms up! Be ready for anything that comes through!"

The light got brighter by the second. All the soldiers were noticeably terrified at the thought of what was about to happen. The ground began to shake when, in a single moment, the light opened into a giant wormhole.

"What is that?" one soldier questioned.

The people who were spectating along the side of the road and in and on top of the buildings couldn't believe their eyes either. They stood motionless in complete fear and anxiety not knowing what to do next. Stay? Watch? Try to get closer? All they knew was that they were in uncharted territory.

"Major," Smith said. "I think we need to step back. Whatever is coming through that wormhole - I highly doubt that it'll be friendly."

Collins nodded in agreement. "Alright, men. Fall back a bit. Keep those guns raised. If anything comes through, light it up! That's an order. Now move!"

As everyone stepped back, hundreds of civilians could be seen gathered on the rooftops all around. The city held silent as the soldiers prepared for what was next. News vans were around every corner trying to get the story. Reporters and camera operators all gathered around to get media coverage at this unprecedented event. Chicago was ground zero for what was, no doubt, the strangest phenomenon in the city's and perhaps, the world's, history.

Smith opened his laptop, pulled out a sensor, and pointed it at the wormhole. As he did that, the rest of the soldiers held their stance ready for anything.

"What are you doing, Lieutenant Smith?" Collins asked.

"It's a thermal scan. I just want us to be ready for anything. If there are any heat signatures, this will pick it up... hopefully. Again, this is uncharted territory, sir."

Just as he said that...

A huge explosion came through the wormhole and with it; an army of strange creatures, reptilian in nature, came through and began attacking the city. The people scattered in a mad dash to get to safety. But the creatures picked them all off one by one tossing them about like rag dolls.

Collins shouted, "Soldiers, attack. Spare nothing that comes through!" He looked over toward Smith. "Lieutenant, can you shut it down?"

Smith looked at his laptop worried. The look on his face made it painfully clear.

"There's no way to close it, sir. Whatever opened it from the other side is keeping it open. I'm afraid we don't have any choice but to fall back... now."

The look on Collins' face spoke a thousand words that were clearly filled with horror. He stood frozen in disbelief. As he stood there, he could see the soldiers under his command falling one by one. The hordes of creatures coming through ripped them apart in a matter of minutes. In an instant, the National Guard was decimated.

"Major!" Smith shouted.

Collins slowly picked up his radio.

"Fall back, men," he said slowly and quietly. "FALL BACK!"

Major Collins picked up his assault rifle and fired directly into the wormhole. He shot off everything he had but it apparently had little to no effect. Noticing that, he looked over and saw that one of the soldiers was still inside one of the tanks.

"Soldier," he shouted, "Fire everything at that hole!"

But just as he gave the command, though, a huge explosion hit directly in front of them and it sent both Smith and Collins flying until, finally, they both landed in the field in front of the school.

All around them was destruction. The city was in ruins. In just a matter of minutes, all of Chicago was destroyed. Buildings, cars, homes... all reduced to ash and rubble. The fire left the city aglow well into the night and all that could be heard throughout the streets were the screams and cries of all the innocent people who were being hurt and had lost everything.

A young woman appeared from the smoke shortly after. "Where's my baby?!" she cried out. She searched for several minutes until she saw a stroller resembling the one her baby was lying in. As she ran over to the stroller, her heart raced in a panic. When she finally reached it, all she could think was, "Please, not my baby."

She flipped the stroller over and found her infant son laying there lifeless. Immediately, she unstrapped the baby and embraced him in her arms. Suddenly, a bright light came up behind her. As she looked back at it, she noticed that it was a wall of fire. Just as she started praying, the fire came and swallowed her up. It left behind no trace of anything in its path.

Collins and Smith were still lying in the field. Just as Collins was about to awaken, a shadowy, hooded man walked past them and stood over Collins. His long, black, leather coat draped down to his ankles and, underneath his hood, the only thing that can be seen was his eyes. They were eyes of pure evil.

He was frightening and ruthless. His moves were cold and calculated as he laid waste to the city. Many more cries for help could be heard as he did the impossible with his fingers, shooting fire and lightning from them. All that Collins could do would be to just lay there as he saw the horror.

The Major tried to muster up within him every bit of strength that he could to get up and fight this evil off, but his efforts proved to be unsuccessful. His body simply couldn't handle the pain from the blast.

He eventually managed to crawl over to Smith as he looked on in horror at the destruction that was wrought on the city. Collins's worst fears were confirmed - Smith was dead along with his entire group of soldiers. They all had fallen along with much of the population. Then, the man spoke...

"You couldn't stop this, Collins...," the figure said. "You don't have the power to stop me. And you'd be foolish to think that you could stop what's to come. This isn't over, and we'll meet again, Major."

He looked up towards the sun as Collins reached up to grab him in one last-ditch effort. Collins was able to rise to his feet to stand up to this man, but then, fell to his knees as he accepted his fate.

"The end of your world has begun..."

He walked away laughing as Major Collins stood powerless to stop him.

CHAPTER 1

For the past two years, the world has been overrun. During the day, the streets remained quiet. Most days, it would be so quiet that you could hear a pin drop. Many people spent their days searching the abandoned buildings looking for whatever supplies they could find. Nights were a different story, however. They were often full of danger and peril. As soon as the sun would set, the world was ablaze. Gangs had taken over certain areas of the city and the innocent never knew when a gang war would rise or where the next bullet would come from. The world had been thrown into complete chaos and Chicago was no exception. And although the conditions that the world dealt with were less than ideal, Chicago would quickly become ground zero for the greatest war that humankind had ever known.

The city was a lot different now than most people remember. What was once a major metropolis, was now almost a wasteland. With the Night-stalkers, a race of mindless, reptilian-like humanoids running the streets, much of humanity had been nearly eradicated. What little was left of the population was driven underground to live out their lives in nothing but fear and terror while the rest lived in rundown homes in many of the neighborhoods. The governments of the world had been completely eradicated so there were no more laws to live by and no order in society. There was only survival, and many preferred to live this life separate from one another because supplies and resources were low and they felt that, to survive, it would be much better to be alone.

No doubt, the Event left the citizens of Chicago, as well as the rest of the world, with plenty of stories to tell. Where many lived in fear, a select few had the courage and bravery - and the power - to end the madness.

"Christian, come on. We gotta move, bro."

"Hold on, D. I think I found something."

Damien Drake and Christian Clarke were best friends. Over the course of the past two years, they became more like brothers having faced many trials together. They were the most unlikely of friends. Prior to this life, Damien was a star quarterback at their high school and a very gifted athlete. Christian, on the other hand, was an aspiring inventor. He kept his head in the books throughout his childhood and it carried on through his teenage years. Even though they went to the same school, they didn't know each until after the Event. That's what the Earth invasion came to be called. In a world of destruction and isolation, they had each other. They were family.

Resources were scarce all around. There were no more businesses to shop from, no stores to make purchases. Survival was the game's name, and it meant, sometimes, raiding old remnants of storefronts and shops to make ends meet, so to speak. While on a supply run, the two of them came across an old convenience store. Anything that they could find that could be used was considered a win. Food, medicine, it didn't matter. Anything would be a plus in their book.

Damien walked over to Christian. "What is it?"

Christian sifted through the dust and debris on the ground. Through the broken glass and ashes, he pulled out a framed picture of a family. It recalled what it was like for him to live with his family before the Event took place. He missed his parents and his brothers and sister. Overwhelmed with emotion, he began to shed tears.

"You alright?" Damien asked.

"Not really," he answered. "Sometimes, I really wish that I could go back in time and change all of this. Let's be honest, this life sucks and I'd give anything to be able to go back and have, at least, one more moment with my family."

Damien chuckled. "Trust me, you're not alone. I get so sick of living like this sometimes. Other times, it's really not too bad, I guess. I did end up getting stuck with you," he said jokingly.

"Real funny," Christian said laughing. He then wiped the tears away and looked up at Damien. "You ever wonder what happened to families like this one?" He stood up and set the picture on the counter. "I mean really wondered if they made it through the destruction together?"

"All the time," Damien answered. "Honestly, I think you have to believe that. You need to have hope in something, Chris. Otherwise, what are we fighting to survive for? This world was already a dark place before all of this. Murders, robberies... It was just bad. Corruption throughout the city. It's crazy that we really thought we were on the right course, though. Somehow, in some way, people as a whole thought that they had it. But people were wrong. But the thing is, somewhere in these days of darkness, there has to be some kind of light."

"Man, I hate it when you're right. Since when did you become a philosopher?" Christian replied. He put the picture in his backpack and looked around. "What all can we get out of here?"

"Mainly, medical supplies," answered Damien. "We need aspirin, antibiotics, and whatever else we can find. We're probably not gonna get another moment like this for a while. Let's load up and get out of here."

Immediately, both men started to sift through the rubble. They made sure to take their time because they didn't want to miss anything that could prove valuable. They moved around dirt, glass, boulders – whatever it took to stock up on the bare necessities.

They spent about forty minutes raiding the entire store. They found canned goods, pain relievers, bandages, and many other items that could be useful and stored them in Damien's backpack. They made one final sweep of the store but decided that they had gathered everything that they needed.

"I think we're good to go here," Damien said. "Let's go. It's almost dark."

As they exited the store, along the streets were people scavenging for meals, going through dumpsters in alleys, and trying to catch rats and pigeons along the way. These were truly desperate times for many. Children ran the streets starving for food and shelter, left alone from the destruction. These two years left everyone in a state of anguish and anxiety. No one was an exception.

"Please, please," they could hear as they walked the street. "Help us!" The people were in pain. They were starving, sick, and dying a slow and painful death. The Event left its mark in a way that most couldn't expect or imagine.

As they were walking, a young boy about twelve years old happened alongside them. "Could you spare anything?" he asked.

Damien took his backpack off without hesitation and reached down in it and pulled out an apple. "These are hard to find, kid. I hope you enjoy it." He then handed the kid the apple and the boy took it and ran off around a nearby corner leaving Christian and Damien to go about their way.

The two men had a long walk ahead of them – about two miles. Along the way, they laughed and talked about what they would be doing if the world was the way it was before the Event.

"It would be my second year of college right now," Christian started. "At least, I'd be getting ready to start right now. You know, I had a full ride for M.I.T. set? I was just getting set to go when all of this happened. My parents were so proud."

"I bet," Damien replied. "I was on my way to Southern Illinois in Carbondale with a football scholarship. Full ride! I had it all planned out. I was supposed to go to school, play football, meet the girl of my dreams, get drafted into the NFL, get married, and see the world. I even had a backup plan just in case football didn't work out. So, I majored in criminal justice. My parents were actually surprised that I had a plan let alone a backup plan. I was never the 'plan ahead' type. But I knew that I wanted to take care of them and my sister."

"See, it was a bit different for me," Christian said. "I didn't know what I wanted to do beyond M.I.T. I just wanted to go to school, invent and build some amazing tech, and get out of Chicago. I guess, I probably would've started some kind of tech company eventually. I always enjoyed making things."

"Yeah, that would've been great, bro, for sure."

As they neared their home, the sun had set. Almost at once, flames could be seen engulfing the city. This was a regular occurrence at night since the power to the city was at a minimum and needed to be preserved.

The nighttime was also the most dangerous. It was then that the worst of the worst came out to terrorize the ones who tried their best to live in peace. These ones were made up mostly of people who escaped the prisons and mental facilities in the area. Over time, some of them formed gangs and did their best to claim territory across the Chicago area. They didn't care who they hurt as long as they took care of their own.

As the two of them neared their home, a faint sound could be heard in the distance. It was the eeriest laugh possible. Almost wicked. At a moment's notice, Damien stopped and put his arm in front of Christian.

"Wait," Damien said. "Did you hear that?"

"Hear what?" Christian looked puzzled. He began to get nervous.

Suddenly, there was a strange silence. Then out of nowhere, Damien is knocked down from behind.

The leader of the group of five stood tall over Damien. "You boys are in the wrong part of town, ain't cha???" His partners closed in with sinister looks on all their faces.

Damien groaned, holding the back of his head, as he got up. "What do you want?" he asks.

The leader smiled with an evil grin before he spoke. "We need your supplies. Whatever you have on ya, we want it, and you're gonna give it to us or we're gonna cut 'cha up real nice, ya understand?"

Damien dropped his backpack to the ground and looked over at Christian. "Get back to the house... now."

Without hesitation, Christian left to go to their home. He wasn't a fighter, and he knew it. So, he did exactly what Damien had told him to do.

Damien, then, looked up at the four following men and then over to the leader. "You want it," as he looked down at the backpack, "come and get it."

The group ran to attack Damien. They had chains, spiked bats, and brass knuckles as weapons, but with every blow that came, Damien took it in stride. After about a minute of just enduring blow after blow he slowly started fighting back - blocking every strike. Then he started to counter every move. Growing bored, Damien began a full-out assault. Each man fell one after the other until only the leader was left standing. He grabbed him by his neck and kicked him in one of his kneecaps with enough force to break it.

"If I catch you around here again, we're gonna have a little party with my boot meeting your face. Got it?!"

With that, the leader got himself up and gathered his thugs and they all started to hightail it out of the area.

"Hey, where are you all going," Damien yelled jokingly. "We were just starting to have fun!" Damien laughed to himself as he picked up the backpack. "Oh well..."

On the surface, he showed no fear, but deep down he knew that situation could go badly very quickly. He knew he was extremely fortunate in that outcome. Nevertheless, he needed to catch up with Christian. So, Damien ran after him to catch up and head back home.

CHAPTER 2

The world after the Event changed forever. The planet was left in a state of complete devastation. As the cities around the world gradually fell, the landscape changed. More and more places became more isolated and desolate. Wooded areas had expanded as the human population decreased at drastic rates and so-called concrete jungles were well on their way to being merged with actual ones.

The scene in Chicago was no different. What was once a sparkling metropolis could only now be described as a mere shadow of what it once was. After two years of population reduction, the forest preserves had spread out into the main parts of the surrounding areas. With no one around to keep up the maintenance, everything had begun to fall apart. Countless businesses were lost across the city. There were no more stadiums for sporting events, no concert venues, and no restaurants... Absolutely nothing was left.

Since these things were gone now, most people only felt hopelessness or despair. Where was the entertainment to brighten up their darkened days? What would they do without that next big concert of their favorite music artist or something as simple as enjoying the everyday, excitement of binge-watching their favorite television show? The simple things that everyone once took for granted were now gone, perhaps, forever. But out of all of that, the people lost the one thing that meant represented a sense of security - their homes.

There were no more neighborhoods. No communities were left. Parks and schools were all destroyed. Some had set up small shelters around the city to assist in placing people after the Event, but most were left living on either the streets or in abandoned homes. Somehow, though, in a world that seemed so dark, there was always a way for the light to shine through.

Damien and Christian reached their home shortly after. It wasn't much. Just an abandoned, old house in one of the old neighborhoods. Since the Event, resources such as electricity and natural gas had been scarce. So, whenever they could, they would charge up a couple of generators that they had managed to salvage in order to keep the power on and they used electric heaters and blankets to keep warm at night.

Once they walked into the house, Damien dropped his bag at the table and sat down to take a minute to himself. "What's in here to eat? I'm starving."

Christian walked into the kitchen, looked in the cabinet, pulled out a couple of cans of food, and held it up. "Creamed corn or pork and beans?"

"No meat? There's nothing in the freezer?" Damien asked.

Christian went to the refrigerator to check it out. "There's not much in here, honestly. Mostly vegetables and we barely have that. Let me go check the trap outside."

He walked out around to the back yard where they had several bear traps set up.

Empty...

"Well...," Damien said, "I guess pork and beans and creamed corn it is. I'll be honest, though. I sure could go for a steak right about now."

"Yeah, tell me about it," Christian agreed. "A ribeye with a loaded baked potato sounds really good. You know, I wouldn't mind running a farm just so we could get some of those things again. Even if we had tried to set up a garden out back, seeds are difficult to come by now."

"Picture that! Christian Clarke, a farmer," Damien exclaimed as he laughed out loud. "Maybe one day, Chris. One day, we can have the life that we had before. You're a genius. If anyone can figure it out, you can."

As they ate their dinner, the sun had begun to set. This was usually a critical time every evening because that was when the danger was at its highest, even in the suburban area south of Chicago, where they lived. It was almost as if day and night were two different worlds. The howls of wolves, owls, crickets, and other creatures filled the sounds of the night as the wind blew overhead.

As the night went on, Damien grew more and more restless. Unable to sleep, he got up and sat outside on the front porch and gazed at the clear night sky. Where he came from as a young, bratty kid from the suburbs of Chicago was a far cry from where he was now. In just two short years, he changed so much in responsibility. He was wiser and more in tune with himself and who he was as a person. He, with Christian's help, overcame all the adversity and grew as a man. Yet, on the inside, he was deeply troubled and emotionally scarred.

On this particular night, Damien felt more uneasy than usual. His dreams were full of fire, lightning, and pure rage. To him, it seemed as if something almost sinister was attempting to break through and that it would be something he couldn't control. Damien felt, deep down, that something was on the horizon waiting for him and he could not avoid it. But it was just a feeling. After a while, Damien decided to lie back down to get a bit of rest.

Once the morning came, it was time to get back at it. The daily grind of finding food and supplies was a regular routine. Christian was always the one to get up first. He would plan the routes and supply lists down to the smallest detail. That was his specialty. Damien on the other hand acted more as a guardian to Christian since the Event. Since he was a fighter and was older, he saw Christian as a younger brother and felt protective of him. After eating breakfast, they sat at the table to discuss their plans.

"Today, we need to head east past Green Lake Woods to the old River Oaks Mall," Christian started. "I figure we can get supplies like some electronics and maybe some clothes and gear. We might be able to stock pretty well there since, if I'm not mistaken, has been largely untouched."

"That's because it's been crawling with those things," Damien disputed. "Especially since the trees and the wildlife started taking over. It's a hunting ground. We'll never make it out, and that's if we manage to make it in."

"It's risky," Christian said, "but right now, this may be our best chance to score big for a while. We won't need to restock anytime soon. I think it may be worth it."

Reluctantly, Damien agreed. He gathered everything that he thought they would need for the trip: first aid, weapons, and a radio. Christian sat and studied the map of the area thoroughly enough to where he was able to navigate possible trouble routes and exit points. After a few minutes, they were both ready to go. As they both got up and were ready to leave, they heard a large branch break outside.

"Did you hear that?" Christian questioned. "Something just hit the ground with that branch."

"I'll go check it out," Damien said.

Damien stepped outside to investigate the area, looking around to find the fallen branch. As he was walking, he heard a faint moan through the wind. At first, he thought that he was hearing things. But then, he heard it again.

"Help... help!" the voice cried out.

Damien ran in the direction of the voice and, to his surprise, found a young boy lying in the snow hurt.

"Kid?" Damien said. "Kid, you alright?"

"Yeah, I'll be ok."

As the boy tried to get up, he fell right back to the snow and screamed out in agony.

"That doesn't look like 'ok', kid. Let me check it out."

Damien examined the kid's legs to assess the problem. No broken bones. No blood.

"Alright. It just looks like it's sprained. You'll be fine. We just gotta get that ankle wrapped up."

The kid agreed as Damien picked him up and took him into the house. Once they got inside, Damien sat him down on the floor and rushed to get the medical supplies to wrap his ankle up.

Christian looked up. "So, what happened?"

"That's what this young man is going to tell us," Damien answered. He looked over to the kid. "Aren't you? What were you doing out there, kid? Don't you know it's not safe to be out there by yourself?"

"I know," he answered in a somber voice. "I was just looking for some food. I'm hungry."

"What were you planning on finding in that tree?" Christian asked.

"I don't know. Something..." The kid looked away and held his head down.

"Hey kid," Damien said. "What's your name?"

The kid looked up at both Damien and Christian. "James. But my friends call me Jimmy."

Damien and Christian formally introduced themselves and offered him something to eat. They didn't have much but, in this world, what doesn't seem like much can be everything to one person, especially a child.

As Jimmy ate, Christian tried to find out a little more about their young guest as Damien got the rest of the supplies ready for their trek through the snowy wilderness. As it turned out, Jimmy wasn't too much different from them. He recently became an orphan due to the attacks in the city. Since then, he had taken to the streets to fend for himself. It was a hard life indeed.

Damien looked over at them. He said to Jimmy, "We can't leave you by yourself. I'll be honest with you. Where we're going is dangerous. But I'm afraid that if we leave you here alone, you might be worse off than taking you with us. I need to know if you can handle this, kid."

Jimmy responded, "I'm good. I can handle it."

"Good," Damien said. "If you two are ready, it's go time. If we're gonna make a move, now's the time."

"Can you walk?" Christian asked Jimmy.

He nodded his head in agreement as he finished his food.

As they walked out, Damien looked down at Jimmy. "From now on, kid, you stick with us. We'll take care of you. You go where we go, and you sleep where we sleep. We're family now. This is your home. Cool?"

Jimmy smiled at them and answered back, "Cool."

Damien and Christian picked up their backpacks and the three of them, together, headed out to face the day.

CHapTer 3

Daytime in Chicagoland is usually pretty quiet, and peaceful. The people didn't roam the streets too much anymore and, when they did, it was always quick trips outside and then back in. Gone were the days of children going outside to play with their friends or a family taking a day trip to the park for a picnic and fun. Times were certainly different, and the people longed for another time when they could live in peace again.

The nighttime held a different type of danger lurking in the streets. It was something far more primal, more deadly. They came to be called Night-Stalkers. These were humanoid creatures, reptilian in nature, who only came out when the sun had set. For the last two years, they would come from under the cover of the night sky to terrorize the city and all of its inhabitants making Chicago a very scary place to be at night. No one knew what they were exactly other than the fact that they came through the wormhole during The Event.

While walking through the city, Damien and Christian took the time to get to know Jimmy a little more. At the same time, Damien stayed ever watchful, always minding his surroundings. That was something that Damien excelled in – being a protector, a guardian. After watching over and protecting Christian for the past two years, having Jimmy come in made him feel like his life had a little more meaning than just fighting to survive.

"You alright?" Christian asked.

Damien continued to look around. "You ever had the feeling you were being watched?"

"D, that is so cliché, bro," Christian said. "This ain't a horror movie."

But Damien felt extremely uneasy. "I don't know. Something just doesn't feel right. It's like I can feel something. It's giving me the heebie-jeebies and I don't like it."

Jimmy looked up at him. "You'll be OK, Damien."

They kept moving along throughout the woods, traversing through what used to be Calumet City. Without as many people around, it became a wasteland full of trees and dilapidated buildings. Eventually, after over an hour of walking, they arrived at the old River Oaks mall. The scene was quiet and quite abandoned. This was the first time in a year and a half that anyone was brave enough to travel through the area due to a high concentration of Night-Stalkers in the vicinity.

They got inside the mall by breaking the glass in the doors. As they got inside, they could see rats and raccoons racing across the floor, scrambling and searching for food.

"We're gonna walk through here?" Jimmy immediately questioned.

"See, Chris," Damien started. "Even the kid thinks this is crazy."

The stores all remained mostly intact. Everything was left just as it was two years ago during The Event except for some slight decay. But the important thing was what was left behind. Countless stores were filled with clothes, shoes, and even some electronics.

They began their search near the food court, slowly sifting through a nearby clothing store. Christian took the lead in the search, charging from one store to the next. He picked up whatever he felt could be useful. It didn't matter what it was. Jimmy stayed by Damien's side as he kept watch.

"Are you brothers?" Jimmy asked.

"Nah, kid," he answered. "Not by blood at least. You could say we became brothers over time."

Jimmy held his head low. "I lost my brother."

Damien could feel the pain in Jimmy's voice. He crouched down beside him. "You know, kid? I lost some people close to me, too. So did Christian. We all did. That's why I stick close to Chris. So, I don't lose him, too. And guess what? You won't lose us either. You'll always have a home wherever we go."

It was only a few words. But those few words were more than enough to calm Jimmy's unsteady mind and heart. All was calm for a while, until...

"Damien!!!" Christian ran over to get Damien's attention.

"What is it?"

"Bro, you gotta see this."

Damien followed Christian over to the store in the next wing of the mall. When they got inside, Damien couldn't believe his eyes. It was several small children living inside this one store all ranging in age from thirteen down to three. The situation was so grim for some of the kids that it brought Christian to tears. Damien immediately stepped in to try to give the children comfort. But they were so afraid that with each step closer that Damien took, the children would step back.

Damien, realizing the fear of the children, called Jimmy over. "Try to talk to them, Jimmy. Reassure them. Let them know that they're safe."

Jimmy walked up to the children and knelt down in front of them. Damien and Christian just stood back watching, waiting. As Jimmy knelt down, he took the hand of one of the children and looked him in the eye. When he did that, the young boy, at first, shivered in fear. But Jimmy didn't let go. He held on tightly until the boy felt comfortable.

"It's ok," Jimmy told him. "It's alright. They're here to help. You can trust them."

The young boy got up and walked over to Damien. Damien got down on one knee to make the boy feel comfortable and they looked each other in the eyes. Damien gave the young child a slight head nod to reassure him that everything was, indeed, going to finally be alright. Almost immediately, the boy felt a major sense of relief. He knew in his heart that the storm was over. Damien, then, picked the boy up and walked over to Christian.

"Alright, Chris," Damien started. "We can't just leave them here."

"I know," he responded. "It's too dangerous for them to be alone. They're too young. Only babies."

Christian stopped for a second to think. "I think I saw a truck sitting outside. We could move them in that. It's definitely bigger than the one we drove out here."

Damien nodded in agreement. Christian sat his bag down and headed toward the door. Damien signaled to Jimmy to start rounding up all of the children to get ready to move. Damien, looking on, thought to himself about the road ahead. How will they care for these children, much less, keep them safe from the everyday threats of the world? Just as Jimmy finished getting the kids together Christian ran back in.

"Damien!" Christian yelled. "Damien!" He ran up to Damien short of breath. "D, we got a serious problem."

Damien followed Christian outside and much to his surprise, it was an army of Night-Stalkers... in broad daylight!

"What in the world are they doing?" Damien wondered as he thought out loud.

Christian looked back at the mall thinking about the young children on the inside. "I don't know. But we definitely have to get them out before they get too close."

"Go inside and get everyone together," Damien said. "Get them out of here as soon as possible. I'll try to hold them off. If you have to leave without me, do it. Just get them all to safety."

"No, we leave together," Christian demanded adamantly. "We don't split up."

"There's no time. I'll catch up."

Christian looked at Damien with uncertainty, not knowing if he was making the right decision. Damien gave him the same reassuring nod that he gave to Jimmy just minutes before and Christian ran back inside to gather the children. Once Christian arrived safely inside, Damien charged toward the Night-Stalkers.

Once Christian got inside, he locked the doors and rushed to the young ones. "OK, kids. We're moving now. We gotta go."

Jimmy walked over to Christian and whispers, "Is everything OK?"

Christian just looked at Jimmy and, immediately, Jimmy knew that there was trouble outside. Soon after, they started to move the kids toward the door.

Meanwhile, Damien reached the band of Night-Stalkers intent on starting the fight of his life. He couldn't help but wonder to himself if he would even survive. He dropped his coat to the ground and revealed a small armory attached to him. Guns, knives, grenades... Whatever he needed was at his disposal.

As they approached, the Night-Stalkers let out a loud screech and, in the process, shattered several windows. Damien stood thinking to himself which was worse: their scream or their appearance. The Night-Stalkers each stood approximately six feet tall with long tails with spikes on their ends. Their faces were all scarred with slimy skin and razor-sharp teeth. Their bodies were all heavily armored with thick scales. And to make matters worse, there were a total of seven of them versus just Damien. He, no doubt, had his work cut out for him.

Damien, not one for stepping down from a challenge, began to charge. He raised the machine gun on his hip, took aim, and fired. One fell immediately leaving six more. Once he got in closer, he let the machine gun fall to his waist and pulled out two enormously large army knives. Once he got in close quarters, he slashed away. Each of the remaining creatures put up a strong fight... but so did Damien.

Back at the mall, Christian and Jimmy worked together to get everyone out and to safety. Christian ran outside to the truck and started to hot wire it to start. Once it finally started, he signaled for Jimmy to start bringing the children out. One after the other, the kids bolted out of the mall and piled into the truck to steer clear of the danger.

"Come on, everybody," Christian shouted. "We have to move!"

It took a few minutes, but eventually, everyone was loaded into the truck. Once all of the children were secured, all that was left was for Jimmy to get in. But as he is coming out of the building, another Night-Stalker jumped down in front of him and blocked his exit. The only thing that Christian could think to do was to throw a punch at it. But the creature caught the punch and began to squeeze his hand, breaking him down. The monster then picked Christian up by the neck with its tail and, with a sinister grin, started punching him furiously in the stomach.

Christian was defeated easily. The creature then raised its fist high to the sky drawing back a powerful blow to finish him off. But out of nowhere from behind was a mysterious, old man in tattered clothes with a hood covering his face. He quickly grabbed the monster's arm, broke it twice, and with his bow staff, impaled it.

"Are you alright, young man," the old man asked.

Christian looked up at the old man for a second then looked back down. "I'm fine. Thank you."

When Christian looked up, the old man was gone.

Meanwhile, Damien still had his hands full fighting the remaining Night-Stalkers. He put up a strong fight, but the sheer power and stamina of the monsters proved to be too much. Soon, fatigue took over and Damien's fight neared its bloody end. The Night-Stalkers began to easily overpower him, eventually rendering him unconscious. As quickly as the fight began, it ended – ended with Damien lying helpless in the middle of the street.

Suddenly, out of nowhere, the hooded, old man showed up and sounded off a horn that frightened the last of the Night-Stalkers, scaring them away. He, then, walked over to Damien, picked him up, and carried him back to the mall parking lot where Christian, Jimmy, and the rest of the children were ready to move out.

The old man looked over at Christian. "He's hurt pretty badly. We have to get to safety before more come. I have a place where we can go so that we'll be safe. Just follow my directions carefully."

"That's fine," Christian responded. "But we've gotta get these kids somewhere they won't get hurt."

"It's taken care of. Let's just get out of here."

With that, Christian started up the truck without a problem, looked back at an unconscious Damien, and they drive off to safety yet, still, waiting for the unknown.

CHAPTER 4

S ilence filled the air as they drove. They had been on the road for over twenty minutes riding along the expressway and not a single word had been said. With Damien lying in the back of the truck unconscious and this mysterious person sitting next to him, Christian couldn't help but be nervous.

So many thoughts filled his mind during the drive. Would Damien be alright? Where were they going? Would the children, in fact, be safe? Who was this mysterious person that they all made this escape with? So many questions to be asked but not nearly enough answers. After a while, Christian couldn't take the silence any longer. So, he decided to attempt to break the ice.

He turned and glanced over at the man. "Thank you," he said. "Seriously, thank you. We'd all be dead if it wasn't for you."

"You're welcome." The man looked up at the signs on the expressway and after several more miles, he directed Christian. "Get off at this exit. Once you do, you'll turn left."

Christian turned the truck and headed down a dark road in old downtown Chicago just as the sun began to set. As he was driving, all of those questions continued to eat away at him. He absolutely needed to know.

"Who are you?" he asked. "You came out of nowhere and saved us all. Don't get me wrong, I'm grateful. But you haven't spoken a single word since we left the mall and, quite frankly, it's freaking me out."

The man continued to look straight ahead and answered, "My name is Cyris."

"OK, great. We're getting somewhere," joked Christian. But things got very serious very quickly. "Where did you come from though? Where did you learn to fight like that? And why were those Night-Stalkers out in broad daylight?"

Cyris took a deep breath and said, "Look, I understand you have a lot of questions. But right now, you need to just focus on driving. We'll be at our destination soon. Then, you'll get your answers."

"Cool. What about the kids, though? Will they be fine where we're going?"

Cyris gave him a reassuring nod and they kept driving.

As they drove, Christian took in the sights. It was downtown Chicago. A place once filled with life day in and day out. But what was once a bustling metropolis could only be seen now as an almost completely barren wasteland. Many buildings now lay desolate and near total ruin. Most of the skyscrapers that filled the Chicago skyline were nothing more than empty, rundown buildings.

"Man, it's crazy," Christian mused. "I was here the day it all happened. Earlier that day, I mean. I was here with my parents. We were here walking down this exact street. It's crazy how quickly things can change. Now they're not here."

Cyris just turned and looked out of the window. He took a deep breath. "So was I. I saw it all. That morning was just a normal morning. Next thing I know, it turned out to be the worst day of my life – along with everyone else's." Noticing where they were,

Cyris gave more direction. "We're here. Turn right on Jackson Blvd. and go down to the lower-level parking garage at the old federal building."

Christian continued driving until they reached the building. They entered the garage and drove as low as they could.

"Why the federal building?" Christian asked.

As they got out, they gathered all of the children together and directed them to follow the corridor that led to a level below where they were. Cyris quickly commanded the guards to lift Damien out of the back of the truck and, from there, they took him to the infirmary along with the children.

"Before the Event took place," Cyris started, "the building had a top-secret, high-level security military facility located deep below ground. Only a select few people knew about it, me included."

Once they reached the door, Cyris punched in his security code on the keypad and the door opened up to reveal the base that he spoke of. It was like nothing that Christian had ever seen before. Where they walked in led directly to a command center. Dozens of people were gathered in this central chamber. But he hadn't seen anything yet.

"I was one of them," he continued. As they moved through the crowd and down the stairs, Cyris continued to explain. "This facility was used to develop high-tech weaponry to combat the war on terror. Back in the days of groups like Al-Qaeda, ISIS, and other splinter cells, where tactical espionage was still prevalent, this was the place where a lot of new government technology was conceived and brought to fruition. After the Event, I used it as a base of operations of sorts. I put together a small team to fight this threat at the outset. Over the past two years, we've definitely grown in number."

When they finally reached the lowest level, they went through one more door. When they walked through, Christian couldn't believe his eyes.

"It's an entire city down here... beneath the city. It's incredible!"

"It is, isn't it? We call ourselves The Pack," Cyris stated. "We operate as a unit here. We all act in the interest of one another. Down here, we're a family, young man. We're all we have." He turned and looked at Christian and extended his hand and they shake. "You're family now. You, your friend, and all of the children. You all have a home here with us, of course, should you choose to stay."

Almost immediately, a young woman approached Cyris and looked at Christian.

"What happened?" she asked.

"They were ambushed," Cyris answered. "His friend, Damien, tried to fight them all off and got knocked out in the process."

"OK," she responded. "I can assume that he was sent to medical right away?"

"Of course," Cyris answered. "I had a couple of guards take him there as soon as we touched down. We've got a bigger problem on our hands, though. The kid was just fighting anyone. He was fighting Night-Stalkers."

The woman was clearly shaken. "Are you sure? In broad day-light?" Cyris nodded. "If that's the case, I think we need to sound the alarm and have anyone that's outside getting off of the streets immediately."

"Fine. Look, this is Christian. He's Damien's friend."

She shook hands with Christian. "Nice to meet you. Excuse me but there are some more things going on that require my immediate attention. Plus, with the rise in the activity of the Night-Stalkers, we now have to deal with that. We'll talk later."

As she walked away, Christian couldn't help but stare.

"Who is that?" he asked.

"Diamond. She's the leader down here. Come on. I'll show you around. Let's get you something to eat."

Cyris led Christian to the cafeteria until they came to an empty table and sat down. Christian couldn't help but look around in amazement. The level of organization and function left him purely astounded. "About how many people do you have down here?" he inquired.

"Approximately 150. But our numbers are growing. Work began recently to expand the facility upstairs and convert the actual courthouse into apartments for everyone. But with resources running low..."

"...The work stopped."

Cyris continued. "The past two years have been rough on all of us here. Some come from affluent backgrounds and didn't adapt well to the sudden change in circumstances. Being upended from their homes and entire way of life affected them in ways they couldn't possibly imagine. Some chose to adapt. Some couldn't handle the change and killed themselves. Others who either came from poverty or close to it – the so-called middle-class – adapted just fine. I suppose it's all in how you view things. Most have chosen to make the best of a very bad situation."

Christian took in a deep breath and let out a loud sigh. "I suppose we all have to adapt to it." He let out a light chuckle. "You know... When I met Damien, it was right after everything went down. We had lived a few doors down from each other for months and never even knew it. No one knew me really. I was the new guy on the block. A nerd at that. A genius with computers. But not a friend in the world. He found me in the rubble that day. Both of our parents had been killed in the attack. So it's just been us two since then. He's my brother now. I don't know what I'd do without him."

Cyris reassured him, "He'll be alright, Christian. He's strong... Stronger than anyone I've ever known. I can see that." Cyris stood up and began to walk away. "Just watch. You'll see. Make yourself at home. Welcome to The Pack."

As Cyris walked away, Christian couldn't help but wonder what the future would hold. With his friend - his brother - lying unconscious in the infirmary, he couldn't help but be weary of the days that lay ahead.

CHapTer 5

Over the next few days, Christian kept a constant vigil with Damien in the Medical Center. Damien still lay there unconscious after almost a week in the infirmary. The battle with the Night-stalkers took an unforeseen, dramatic toll on his body. Doctors were in and out of the room constantly to check on him – monitoring his vitals and searching for any sign of him regaining consciousness. But so far... nothing.

For the first time in two years, Christian felt alone. The person who saved his life during the Event and numerous times after that - the person who became a friend and brother to him - now lay in a hospital bed helpless. He didn't know how to cope with the situation. Most of his time was spent at Damien's side. When he wasn't with him, Christian spent his time in his room on his tablet doing research and studying.

KNOCK KNOCK...

It was Diamond at the door. "How is he doing? Is he showing any signs of improvement yet?"

"Stable... For now. The doctors are saying that it's about a 50/50 chance of him waking up."

"I hear Dr. Montgomery has been in to see him," Diamond said. "I talked to her just a little while ago. She told me that it looks like he'll pull through."

Christian turned and looked at Damien. "I really hope he does. He deserves it. He fought too hard to get us all to safety for him not to see it all." He took a deep breath and let out a loud sigh. "So, Dr. Murphy, she's good at what she does? I've seen her in here checking on D quite a bit. I'd say just about every time I'm here."

Diamond answered, "She's the best. I can assure you; Damien is in good, very capable hands."

It was only a few words, but Diamond did much to comfort Christian and ease his fears.

Diamond walked into the room and sat down next to Christian and rested her hand on his shoulder. "He'll get up. He's a fighter. I can see that in him, and I haven't had the pleasure of meeting him. Cyris told me about what happened out there. You, Damien, and even little Jimmy - you were all very brave for what you did. Those kids in that mall would've been slaughtered. You saved them. All three of you. So, smile a little."

Christian let out another sigh. "Yeah..."

Diamond noticed the saddened look on his face wouldn't go away. So, she stood up and took Christian by hand. "Come on. You've been down here for days. I know you need a good meal. I insist."

As reluctant as he was, Christian decided to get up and go with her.

"So," he started, "How did you end up down here with The Pack?"

"The day it all happened is pretty much a blur to me. But when I woke up, I was in the care of Cyris. I was bruised up pretty bad.

But he nursed me back to health. It took maybe two months for me to get fully healed."

"What happened to your family?"

"They didn't make it."

"Sorry to hear that. That seems to be a recurring theme these days."

"What do you mean?"

"My parents didn't make it through either. Neither did Damien's. And Jimmy just happened to show up outside our camp about a week ago... alone..."

"I guess it is a recurring theme. I'm sorry for all of your losses."

"How did you become their leader? I mean, no disrespect, but Cyris is much older and from what I've seen, he's a beast when it comes to fighting."

Diamond laughed a bit and they both sat down at the nearest table in the cafeteria. "Yeah, he is definitely a beast when it comes to fighting. He trained me. But he didn't want to lead. It was the responsibility of it all. He just didn't want any of it."

Christian looked on in confusion.

"You see, Cyris lost all of his men to this war. That loss took everything out of him because he felt that he didn't do enough or make enough of the right decisions to keep his team alive. After I recovered, we went out to find any survivors and managed to get a few. We went out every day searching. And at the same time, I trained with him day after day. When we gathered enough people together, I stepped into the leadership role."

Christian asked, "When did this all happen?"

"Two years ago," she said. "The day of the invasion. He led the assault. Lieutenant James Collins. Come on. Lunch is up."

After they ate, they talked for a little while more getting to know each other. It was the most normal either of them felt in a long time. Being in each other's company gave them both a sense of relief and comfort... something that was exceedingly rare in these troublesome times.

"So, tell me more about yourself," Christian suggested.

Diamond chuckled a bit not knowing where to start. "There's not much to me really."

"Not much," Christian questioned. "I doubt it. Tell me about you before all of this."

She struggled at first with her thoughts. Christian caught her off balance with his question. Diamond didn't shy away from it though.

She started, "No one here knows, but before all of this, I was on my high school's cheerleading team."

"Really? Were you any good?"

"Let's just say I wasn't winning the squad any medals," she answered. "I was athletic, sure, but the cheer team wasn't exactly my cup of tea."

"So, what did you wanna do instead?" Christian asked.

Diamond sat back for a moment as if reflecting on that time in her life. "At the time, I don't think that I was really sure. I was still trying to find my way. My parents both tried their best to steer me in the right direction, but I was so lost. I think I always knew in my heart that I wanted to help people. I just wasn't sure how I would do it. Would I be a police officer, a paramedic, or enlist in the military? I just didn't know. It wasn't until The Event that I found out how that would happen. Now I feel my calling is to help people navigate through this war."

"The people seem to be thriving here," noted Christian, "So, you've gotta be doing something right."

"Thanks, but I'm still trying to figure all of this out. Even after two years, we have no clue what it is we're dealing with out there."

Christian reassured her, "The answers will come. 'One day at a time' is what Damien always tells me. So, now I'm telling you."

The way that they connected in an instant was new for Diamond. And she knew it. She hadn't opened up to anyone in that kind of way for the past two years. Christian felt the same way. They each felt a sense of calm and mutual understanding and they conversed for an extensive amount of time.

"Christian!" a voice shouted from afar. It was Jimmy running up to him.

"What's up, little man?"

"How's Damien doing?" he inquired.

Diamond got up and whispered over to Christian. "I'll leave you two to talk. I'll see you later?"

"Yeah, definitely," he replied as he tried to hold back an obvious smile.

As Diamond left, Jimmy sat next to Christian and started to giggle.

"What's so funny?"

"You like her, don't you?" joked Jimmy.

Christian was taken aback by that question and tried to play it off as best as he could. "Boy, moving right along! Yes, Damien is okay. He's still unconscious but it looks like he'll pull through. So, did you make any friends around here yet?"

"I'm working on it," Jimmy said. "Are you sure Damien is gonna be alright?"

Christian gave him a big hug to reassure him. "He'll be fine, little bro. We're family now, kid. I wouldn't lie to you. Come on. I'll take you to go see him."

Christian and Jimmy got up and left the cafeteria to go see Damien. While on the way, Christian noticed the huge smile that was on Jimmy's face.

"You like it here, Jimmy?" he asked.

"Yeah, this place is cool. It's so big! I just can't believe that this is my home now."

Christian smiled and chuckled to himself. He felt the same way that Jimmy did. It was something that he hadn't experienced in a long time. It was an overwhelming sense of solace and having somewhere to belong.

As they reached the clinic, they happened upon Dr. Murphy in the lobby.

"Christian," she called out. "It's good to see you again. I assume you're here to visit Damien?"

"You assumed correctly," he answered. "This time, I brought our friend, Jimmy, with us. I just kinda wanted to show him that Damien was gonna be alright. He hadn't seen him since everything went down."

"Of course," she replied. "Just follow me." As they walked, Dr. Murphy began to explain, "I have to say, he's shown a lot of improvement since he first got here. Hopefully, he'll wake up soon. All of his neural activity is normal and so are his vitals. So, at this point, it's just waiting for his body to jump-start itself. Of course, we want it to happen naturally rather than forcing it just so there's less chance of any setbacks in his recovery."

Christian smiled as they came to Damien's room. "Thank you, Dr. Murphy, for all that you're doing for him."

"It's my pleasure," she answered, "and please, call me Nadia. I'll leave you two alone with him now. Call me if you need me."

With that, Nadia exited the room as Christian and Jimmy sat down next to Damien.

"Is there anything that you wanna say to him?" Christian asked.

Jimmy sat and thought about it for a minute. He then reached over and gave Damien a large hug.

"Thank you," he said as he shed a tear. "Thank you for saving us." As he held onto Damien even tighter, he looked over to Christian. "Do you think he heard me?"

Unsure of what to say, Christian looked at both Damien and Jimmy when the most remarkable thing happened. Damien, at that moment, began to twitch heavily. Christian couldn't believe what he was seeing. Damien had been completely still for so long in his state. They had waited patiently for some sign of life, but it wasn't until that moment that Christian knew everything would be alright.

He smiled at Jimmy. "Yeah, buddy. I think he hears you."

Immediately, with his other hand and without them noticing, Damien clinched the sheets on his bed. Damien was on his way back from the brink of death.

CHAPTER 6

As the days went on everything remained quiet. Diamond stayed hard at work in her office figuring out the next move to make while Cyris trained day and night. In the meantime, Christian continued to stay by Damien's side, ever vigilant in waiting for his best friend to wake up.

Damien's condition did improve over time. Each day looked a little more hopeful. A flinch here. A twitch there. Things finally appeared to go in the right direction. Damien's doctor, Nadia, remained a constant variable in his well-being. She spent hours upon hours watching over him, nursing him back to health. Even when she was off duty, she would spend time with him in his room reading to him and doing everything that she could to make him comfortable.

Christian stood up and began pacing back and forth. Even though Damien did show improvement, he still worried that he wouldn't wake up. Nadia did what she could to ease his worries. But as his friend – his brother – lay in bed helpless, he didn't know what to do.

"Can you stop that pacing, Chris? You're making me nervous," Damien said wearily.

Christian turned around in disbelief. "Finally! You're awake!"

"What do mean, 'Finally?' How long have I been out?"

"Too long! About a week," Christian answered. "Hold on. I'll be right back."

As Christian left the room in complete excitement, Damien sat up still feeling the effects of the sedatives that he was on. He glanced around the room trying to figure out exactly where he was but couldn't quite get his bearings. His vision was blurry, hazy even, and he was still disoriented. Needless to say, though, he had a ton of questions that needed immediate answers.

A few minutes later, Christian came back with Diamond, Cyris, and Nadia. Immediately, Nadia began to check all of Damien's vital signs and any signs of lasting damage.

"Damien," she said, "My name is Nadia and I'm the physician here in the bunker. I'm noticing that your heart rate is still a bit high and irregular. I'm going to draw some blood from you just to make sure we're not missing anything, alright?"

"Sounds good to me, doc," he replied. "Do what you gotta do." That's when it hit him... "The kids in the mall?!"

"They're fine. They're all safe here in the bunker as well," Cyris answered. He then walked up to the side of Damien. "How are you feeling?"

"I'm doing pretty good, I guess, considering I've been out of it for over a week. I'm just glad to be alive. I'm glad to be here... wherever 'here' is."

Diamond stepped in. "You're safe here, Damien. I'm Diamond. This is my second in command, Cyris. Right now, you're about 10 stories underground. We're the leaders of a small group of fighters called The Pack. Cyris brought you, Christian, and all of the children back here after your fight with the Night-stalkers.

I have to say... I'm impressed. You took on seven of them by yourself. That's not an easy task."

Damien laughed. "Yeah, you can say that again. I'm just glad everyone is safe. So what's up? I see it in both of your eyes. You wanna ask something."

"Right now may not be the time," Diamond replied. "It can wait."

"Is any time ever the right time?" Damien asked. "You might as well just ask now, at least, while I'm awake."

Cyris stepped in. "We want you and Christian to join us, Damien," he said. "We're fighting a war, son. There's no denying that. And you and Christian have been doing this for a while now on your own and that's good, too. But we're losing this war. Any moment we could all be wiped out. But you're special, son. To do what you did and make it out alive – it hasn't been done. We can both see that there is truly something special with you."

"In case you missed it," Damien said, "I'm in a hospital bed right now. I'm not sure how useful I can really be once I get better. If I get back to 100 percent..."

Diamond took Damien's hand in reassurance. "We're not asking you to make a decision right this second. It's not an easy choice. But think about it. Regardless of your decision, you're both welcome to stay for as long as you like. But we need someone like the two of you within our ranks helping to make the tough decisions and to help lead these people. I know that it's a lot. I wouldn't be asking if I didn't think that it was necessary. For now, Damien, just concentrate on getting better. We'll leave you alone to rest now. But please, consider it."

With that, Diamond and Cyris left the room. Christian sat down next to Damien and took a deep breath. His heart seemed heavy, and Damien could tell.

"What's on your mind, bro?" Damien asked.

"I'm just relieved that you woke up," Christian said. "It was touch and go for a while. You really didn't show a real improvement until a couple of days ago."

Damien got up and limped around the room. He walked to the door, leaned his back on it, and folded his arms. "What's up with these people? You say we've been here for over a week. Are they legit?"

Christian answered, "They're the real deal, D. They're fighting this war, more than anyone since it all started."

"But where do we fit in, Chris? Do we belong here? Can we really make a difference?"

"I don't know. I really don't. We've made it on our own for this long. I'm sure that we could make it how we've been living for another couple of years. But what I do know is this: the safety, this feeling of ease, that we have right now, it's only temporary. I guarantee, there will come a time when the Night-stalkers and who or whatever it is that's leading them will bring the fight to our door whether we're here or at the camp. We're either gonna take a stand or watch and wait to be taken out. I'm tired of waiting, bro."

Damien walked back over to his bed to lie back down. He let out a deep sigh. "I can't deny it, you made a valid point. Let me think about it, OK." Christian nodded his head in agreement and walked out of the room.

No doubt, Damien had a lot to think about. Not to mention a week's worth of time to catch up and some serious recuperation. That recovery didn't come easy. His idea of recuperating was spending the better part of each day training rigorously. Sometimes, his training lasted for hours on end. Damien made the gym his second home, sometimes sparring with some of the soldiers with only one goal in mind: to get stronger and learn to fight smarter.

Throughout his training, Cyris and Diamond watched closely. Damien was a machine given the way that he trained day in and day out. He wouldn't stop for anything or anyone. Christian checked on him periodically also. After all, he almost lost his "brother." He wouldn't say it out loud, but he feared what life would be like without Damien. Would he be able to survive? That was a question that he wrestled with over that week. It was a thought that would continue to stay with him even throughout Damien's training and recovery. But he knew that Damien was born for this fight. And somehow, Damien knew it, too.

Over a week had passed by, and after some careful thought, Damien decided to go visit Diamond in her office to talk. He had a great deal on his mind over the last few days. So, he felt that a discussion is in order.

Cyris was in the office with Diamond going over resource planning and tactical training for the troops under their command. All of that was put to the side once Damien entered the room.

"Damien," she said, "what can I do for you?"

"I've been considering what you both said... about joining you and your group."

Cyris asked, "You've made a decision, I assume?"

"I have," Damien started. "But before I tell you what it is, I've got to say this." Diamond and Cyris both nodded their heads in agreement. "These things, whatever they are, they took everything from me. My parents, my sister, my home - everything. Everything and everyone that I've ever loved and cared for is gone. They left me with nothing but memories and rage — a rage that I don't even think revenge and cure. But I'm still standing. And through all of the tragedy, I gained a new brother in Christian. I'm thankful for him and thankful that we've found each other. But we've lived on the run; in the shadows. We've spent over two years now scraping together meals and resources just to stay alive. But now... Now, I'm tired of running. I'm sick of living in darkness. It's not fair. Not to me, you, or anyone else in this world who is living in constant fear. It's time to take the fight to them and end this forever but I can't do that alone. There's just no way possible. So yes. I'll join you. I will fight beside you. And if need be, I'll give my life for you. I will fight. I will find the source of this menace and I vow to you and everyone else that I will tear them down until there is nothing left. I will fight and I... will... end this!"

With that Diamond and Cyris reached out to shake Damien's hand and a new alliance was formed.

CHAPTER 7

Over the next few days, Damien trained day and night with Cyris. They knew the dangers that lay ahead probably better than anyone else. So being in top physical condition was the ultimate goal. Sword training, gun training, and physical conditioning became of the utmost importance. And they were committed with no reservations.

They weren't the only ones that stayed busy. Diamond spent countless hours each day drawing up plans and going through them over and over. It was imperative that she didn't leave anything out or to chance. So, she spent time with her top lieutenants to ensure that when a battle broke out, The Pack would be prepared and equipped to handle it.

Meanwhile, Christian spent his time designing new weapons. He stayed in the lab that Diamond had given him. Sometimes, he slept in there, rarely seeing his actual living quarters. Some ideas were failures. Others were near success. But, no matter what, he never quit. Indeed, the stage was beginning to be set for all-out war.

One day, after they finished their training, Cyris and Damien took a moment to go eat at the cafeteria. Waiting in line, Damien took a moment to look around and take ever in. After two years, he had a real home, some structure, and a healthy routine, and it felt great. He had a sense of stability even though he knew, deep down, that the comfort he felt would soon be uprooted. After all, what would be the purpose of all the training if not to prepare to fight in the war?

After getting their food, they sat down at the table and Cyris looked up at Damien.

"You know, son, I'm really glad that you decided to join us. You're definitely far ahead of any of the fighters here. You'll be a great asset here."

"Yeah, well I'm just looking to make a difference. I want this war to end. It's too much suffering, too much chaos. These people here deserve better. The world deserves better."

"And it will end," Cyris said assuring." Of course, we need intel, too. No war can be won if we're fighting blindly. And that's all we've been doing. It's been two years and we still don't know who our enemy truly is."

"Have you guys had a plan in the past?" Damien asked.

"Honestly," Cyris started, "the plan so far has been to just survive. We've been reactive instead of proactive. I'm a soldier, Damien. I served since I was eighteen years old right up until the world took a nosedive and nearly everything and everyone was wiped out. I watched it all happen firsthand. The terror on the people's faces as they watched friends and loved ones die in an instant. Nothing and I mean absolutely, nothing prepares you for that. Not all the basic training and personal training and everything else that you think the military preps you for can get you ready for what we witnessed that day or for what we're going through now. The most that we can do is be thankful for each day that we live and pray to grow old."

As Damien looked in the distance, he could see Jimmy running up to him. "Hey, Damien!"

"What's up, kid? How are you doing?"

"I'm alright," he said. "I've been in school with the other kids."

Damien appeared surprised. "Oh, really?" Then, he looked over at Cyris. "You have a school down here?"

Cyris shrugged his shoulders and grinned. "Hey, the kids have to learn. We try to prepare them for the day we can take back the ground. Someone will have to lead after we all pass on."

"Hmm," Damien says. "That makes good sense. I'm not mad at that at all." Then, he looked back to Jimmy. "I hope you're paying good attention, Jimmy. I'll be checking on you from time to time to make sure you're doing what you're supposed to be doing, OK."

"That's cool, D," he replied. "I just wanted to say thank you for keeping me safe."

"You don't have to thank me for that," Damien responded. "I couldn't just leave you on your own. I told you, you're family now and family looks out for each other."

Jimmy gave Damien a huge hug and ran off to play.

Cyris looked over at Damien. "See. You're already making a difference."

Damien let out a deep sigh. "Like I told him... I couldn't just leave him on his own. It was no big deal."

"It was a big deal to him," Cyris said. "You changed that boy's life. That, my friend, is making a difference. Just watch, Damien. You're going to have a huge impact on everyone here."

Damien and Cyris finished eating their food and got up to leave. As tired as they were, they decided to pick up their training session the next day.

As Damien walked back to his room, he couldn't help but con-template the times that were ahead. "Can I make a difference?

Can anything that I do make a positive impact?" It was immensely pressuring on him. So, his mind stayed focused on things that were to come. When he finally got inside his room, Damien lay in his bed and went to sleep.

With all the things that raced through his mind, Damien had a rough night's sleep. The next morning, when he got up, he decided to get his day started right away to take his mind off things. So, he got in the shower, got dressed in his workout gear, grabbed his bag, and headed straight for the training room. When he got there, he found Cyris training with Diamond. Christian was present, also, along with Jimmy.

"I see the gang's all here," Damien joked. "We're gonna do one big spar this morning?"

Diamond looked over at Damien. "I don't think you're up to that challenge, doll."

Damien grinned, dropped his bag, and ran to join the spar. "Give me what you got then... doll."

Immediately, they began to fight. Damien began with a running punch which was dodged right away and countered by Diamond. Their blow-for-blow sparring lasted for minutes until someone landed a punch. Diamond first... followed by a counter from Damien. Overhead punches, kicks, uppercuts, hooks. The spar was indeed fierce. But they both enjoyed it.

Not long afterward, Cyris was eager to join in to take on the two of them. With ease, he battled them both. At times, he fought with his eyes closed. Sometimes with one hand behind his back exposing their weaknesses with ease. After knocking them both down, he walked to the wall case and grabbed a practice bow staff. "Choose your weapons," he told them. They got up from the floor and rushed to the wall case to pick their weapons of choice. Diamond chose a set of sai – a blunt knife-like weapon that balances both offense and defense. Damien, on the other hand, chose a set of dual practice katanas.

The two warriors fought with everything they had, but in the end, it wasn't enough. Cyris was able to take them on effortlessly. He matched them with every move that they made to the point of frustrating them both. "Focus! Work together," he told them. But their efforts failed, and within minutes, they were easily beaten.

"You lost because you lack focus," Cyris told them as he helped them both up from the floor. "Coordinate your efforts. Always stay focused. Teamwork. You can't get too comfortable or too confident. That's the only way we can win this war." Looking at their weapons, he said to them, "Diamond, you were using a weapon that is all about defense. Use that as your enemy attacks. Damien, your weapon was a good mixture of offense and defense. The katana is a graceful weapon. You can't use it as if you're swinging your fists like the brawler. As Diamond holds the defense, you come in with the attack. You both are capable of so much more, but the two of you need to learn to work together. For now, get some rest. We'll pick this up tomorrow." With that, Cyris left the training room.

Diamond looked over to Damien and took the katanas to put them away. "You're skilled, Damien. It was fun." She glanced at the distance behind Damien. Christian and Jimmy both stood in the background spectating. "I'll catch you boys later," she said with a smile. "I have to head back to the office."

As she headed out, Damien walked over to Christian and Jimmy and gave them a big hug.

"That was awesome," Jimmy exclaimed as he gave Damien a high five. "Can you teach me some of your moves?"

Smiling, Damien looked down at Jimmy and told him, "One day, kid. For now, though, don't worry about the fighting. Stay in your books. Deal?"

Jimmy nodded his head in agreement. After that, they all left the training room. As they walked, Christian and Damien started talking and catching up on recent goings on in their lives.

"So...," Damien began. "What's up with you and Diamond though, bro?"

Christian was caught off guard. He straightened out his glasses and cleared his throat. "Um... nothing. Why would you ask that?

"Bruh! Come on," Damien said. "This is me you're talking to. You didn't think I'd notice? The whole time we were sparring you could barely keep your tongue in your mouth."

"Shut up! God, I swear I can't stand you sometimes," Christian said laughing. "Yes, I like her but I'm just a regular computer geek. I doubt she's even noticed me or would be interested in getting to know me. I think I can save myself the embarrassment."

"Well, you make her notice, Chris. You get her attention and you let her know what you feel, bro. Look, in these times, we all need a little love. I don't have that opportunity. I would give anything right now to feel the affection of a woman. But you, bro... it's right in front of you. All you need to do is just reach out and grab it. And when you get it, never let it go. This war we're fighting, it takes a lot out of all of us. All I'm saying is that, sometimes, we all need someone we can come back to. Someone to share our deepest insecurities with. Someone to make love to and cuddle with at night. Otherwise, what are we fighting for?" Damien reached over to Christian and hugged him. "I love you, lil' bro. But don't let fear beat out your love for this woman. Go get her." With that, Damien walked away.

Christian looked up at Damien. "What about you? You need love too, Damien."

"When I find it, Chris," he said, "I'll be ready." Damien continued walking off.

When Christian got back to his room, he couldn't help but think long and hard about what Damien said to him. Should he hold back? Should he say how he felt? When was the right time? Is there a right time? The questions just kept flooding his mind. He just didn't know. One thing was for certain, though. He was falling headfirst in love.

Meanwhile, when Damien got back to his room, he got in the shower. As he showered, he began to have flashbacks of the day of the event. His mom, his dad, his sister, all the losses that he endured... A flood of emotions came to him all at once; the anger and pain, the sadness that he felt came to be too much for him to bear. So, he just stood under the shower head to let the water wash away his tears.

After he left the shower, Damien decided to relieve stress by doing some light exercise. He wanted to do anything to take the edge off his emotions. The only thing he knew was to stay active. Over the next hour, he did numerous repetitions of push-ups, sit-ups, and other various forms of exercise. But he didn't get tired. The adrenaline that rushed through his veins, burning bright like a raging fire, kept him energized and alert. But after a while, Damien felt that he had had enough.

When he finally got in bed, he began to sleep almost immediately. Everything was well and quiet until, while he was in a deep sleep, Damien began to convulse violently as if having a seizure. Foam started running from his mouth as the convulsions seemed to have gotten worse. Then, his body began to illuminate with a pale, but distinct, red aura as if he was releasing some kind of energy from his body. As the convulsions stopped, his body slowly began to levitate off the bed until he was high above the bed. The ground began to shake and then... DROP!!! Damien plummeted deep into the bed, waking him up.

He had never been more confused in his life. What had just happened to him? As the sweat was dripping from his face, he sat at the side of the bed thinking, "What in the world is happening to me?"

CHAPTER 8

After sleeping the night away, Damien rose to take a long shower. Still confused as to what happened the night before, he thought it best to ignore it – at least, for the time being - and go about his day.

"Maybe I'll hit the gym later," he thought to himself. After all, the extra workout would've helped to blow off some of his stress. Damien got out of bed finally after contemplating his day and went to the bathroom to get started. He stood in the mirror for a minute and stared at himself until he decided to splash some water on his face to wake himself up. He put his face down inside the sink bowl to wet his face. Once he lifted his head and looked back at the mirror, he thought he saw a skull engulfed in flames in his place. Startled, he jumped back into the wall behind him and allowed himself to regain his composure. He looked in the mirror once more, but everything appeared normal. "Man, I'm losing it," he thought to himself.

Figuring it would help, he turned the shower water on hot to relax his mind and relieve his tension. He washed and stood in the shower under the water for several minutes contemplating his future and whether or not he would have the ability to protect those around him unlike when the Event happened, and he was powerless to do anything to protect his parents and sister. It weighed on him heavily because he didn't want anyone else to meet the same fate that his family had.

He stood in the shower a while longer and that allowed him to relax a bit more. After getting out, he dried off, got dressed, and sat in the chair across from his bed. "What's going on? Am I alright? What's happening to me?" He couldn't help but wonder. Damien reached over to pick up the phone to dial Christian. As he picked up the phone, he noticed something very strange... the phone line was dead. No dial tone or clicking could be heard. Only silence. Confused, he kept trying to dial out but there was no doubt that there was a disconnection. So, he grabbed his coat and bag and headed out of the door.

Once he exited his room, the first thing that Damien noticed was the eerie silence throughout the complex. There were no voices to be heard, no kids running through the hallways playing, and no life throughout the entirety of the complex. It was as if everyone picked up overnight and abandoned the facility. As he made his way down the corridor, the lights flickered on and off. It was so quiet that all that could be heard was the electricity flowing through the lights themselves. As the lights flickered off one last time, Damien reached into his bag and drew out his dagger, and began to creep through the halls, preparing himself for whatever may come.

The first place that he went to was the cafeteria, thinking that everyone might go there in case of an emergency. But when he got there, all he found was silence and an empty room. He searched around for a while in the kitchen and the dining hall, but there was no one left in sight.

The more Damien looked around, the more he felt in his body that something was amiss. He had an uneasiness that sent chills throughout his body leading to a fear that he might be the last person alive throughout the entire complex. Worse still, was the fear that he somehow slept through it all.

Damien continued to search for clues as to what happened, but after a while, he turned up almost nothing. His stomach turned at the thought of everyone's fate. Just as he was about to leave the cafeteria, he heard footsteps coming down the hall accompanied by a faint, low growl. It was a sound that he was all too familiar with: the Night-stalkers.

Immediately, he looked around to find somewhere to hide. That's when he noticed a large beam leading to the ceiling. So, he ran to it and climbed to the ceiling to get a decent vantage point. As soon as he reached the ceiling beams, a single night-stalker walked in growling and snarling. The mindless creature took its time destroying the dining area turning over chairs and crashing the tables.

The creature then made a roar just as Damien dove from above, coming down with his dagger to attack. As the blade pierced the creature's armor plating on its shoulder, it bellowed out another roar that shook the very foundations of the compound. Damien held on with everything he had, digging in further, as the night-stalker jerked violently for him to release. Once he removed the blade, blood sprayed outward as Damien jumped back, knocking it down to the cold, concrete floor.

Once Damien gained his footing, the monster picked itself off the floor, looked at Damien, snarled at him, and went on the offensive. Damien, being quicker, dodged its attack and sliced away at its back further angering the beast. Wasting no time, Damien switched from defense to offense releasing a barrage of melee attacks on the night-stalker. All at once, his anger, his fear, his sorrow, and his regrets, all poured out into a fury of an assault that eventually left the beast bloodied on the floor near death. "This is for my family," he declared as he plunged his dagger through its heart, twisting the blade. "My old and new family..." After regaining his breath, he got up and left.

After leaving the cafeteria, the next stop was the training room. It was a complete contrast to the appearance of the cafeteria. The training room was left in shambles. Most of the weapons lay on the floor, broken into hundreds of pieces. There were large holes in the walls, lights that had fallen to the floor and ignited a massive fire, and it filled the air with a thick cloud of smoke. The heat was so violent and intense. It brought him back to the moment of his parents dying and being unable to get to his sister to save her. It sent a rush of emotions flooding through his body that he couldn't shake. "It's happening again," he thought, feeling helpless all over again as he made his way through the fire and across the room.

In the distance, Damien could hear a faint moaning. He dropped his dagger and bag and rushed over to see who it was. When he got there, he saw that it was Diamond buried underneath the rubble. Her entire body had been pinned underneath one of the heavy metal beams that fell from the ceiling and a pile of stone rubble.

"Hold on, Diamond!" he exclaimed.

It took every ounce of his strength to lift the first piece off. Diamond lay there beaten, bruised and bloodied, and barely conscious. There was nowhere for her to go, no moves to be made.

"Diamond, I'm here. Come on. I need you to wake up!"

She could barely open her eyes, but she knew the voice. "Damien, you have to get out of here," she pleaded. Diamond coughed up blood as she struggled to speak. "Please, you have to leave."

"I'm not leaving without you. You can make it," Damien said. He attempted to lift the debris off Diamond, but it was too heavy.

"Damien," she said. "It's no use. You've gotta listen to me." She grabbed his hand and started crying. "Their army is too strong. We couldn't stop it. The Night-stalkers ripped through here and killed everyone." Tears ran down her cheek as she continued. "They started with the children and then moved on to everyone else. Cyris and I made a last stand here, but it just wasn't enough. We couldn't stop it. They were too much."

"But how, though? How did they know we were down here? I don't get it."

"I don't know, Damien. But they found us, and they slaughtered us like cattle. They slaughtered us like PIGS! But Damien... what's more important is that their attacks were coordinated. They were systematic. They knew exactly where and how to hit us. Someone or something was leading them."

Damien sat confused. "Leading them? Are you sure?"

"It was a man... a man in a black coat and hood. His eyes were glowing a faint red. I could sense the evil in his heart," she said. She started coughing up more and more blood. "Damien, you have to stop him! You have to..."

Diamond died holding Damien's hand. Her last words and breath lingered on Damien's mind for a few minutes before he mustered up the strength to finally lift the rubble from off her. With tears in his eyes, he laid her lifeless body along the wall and began to gather the bodies of all the rest to lay them alongside her - including Cyris, Christian, and even little Jimmy.

Rage began to fill his heart. The thought of his friends laying there slain consumed him with a wave of uncontrollable anger. In an instant, he picked up his bag and dagger, wiped the tears from his eyes, and stormed out. Running towards the exit, he thought of the unimaginable horror that his comrades went through. When he finally reached the top of the stairwell, he kicked the door down and ran out in the open.

"I'm here!" he yelled. "Come and get me!"

The howl of the Night-stalkers could be heard in the distance. Then, out of nowhere, one leaped onto his back and began gnawing at him relentlessly. Damien fought with all the strength that he could muster and flipped the creature to the ground and snapped its neck. Afterward, an army of Night-stalkers charged at Damien. As they attacked, Damien sliced them with his dagger one by one. Limb after limb fell to the street as the Night-stalkers became victim to his blade. Five, ten, twenty, thirty... Damien kept fighting until all of them were finally defeated.

"Is that all?! Show yourself! Why are you hiding?!"

Nothing but the sound of the wind screaming between the buildings could be heard. Then, just as Damien was about to walk away, he felt a tap on his shoulder.

As soon as he turned around... WHAM!

With one hit, Damien had been knocked to the ground. When he looked up, he saw that it was the hooded man that Diamond had described.

"You..." Damien managed to eke out.

"Yes, Damien. Me," he replied in what could only be described as a sinister tone.

"You killed them! All of them! Why?!"

"It doesn't matter, Damien. None of this matters. These people you swore to protect, it's pointless. It doesn't matter."

"What do you mean 'It doesn't matter'? Those were innocent people. Women... children... You slaughtered them all!"

"It doesn't matter because they were all dead anyway. From the moment I set foot on this ground, they were in their graves. They just didn't know it yet. Living on the borrowed time that you all had. There was never any hope for salvation. You thought you were safe in your little bunker? You made it easy for me. Nothing more than fish in a barrel."

He lifted Damien off the ground one-handed by his neck and blasted him right through his stomach with a ball of lightning from his other hand. His eyes began to glow a fiery red under his dark hood. It was just as Diamond had described. They were eyes of pure terror. As he stared Damien down, Damien saw a horror that he never would've imagined. An evil stare that shined through a tattered skull mask. Then he looked Damien in his eyes. "And now, you die along with the hope of this world." He used the hand inside of Damien to shoot an energy blast of fire through him, killing Damien instantly.

He threw Damien's lifeless body to the ground and a great earthquake occurred. Soon after, the sky went completely black, and then...

Damien woke up in his bed in a cold sweat. As he got up to regain himself, he tried to make sense of it all. Was it just a dream? Was it something more? One thing he knew for sure, though, was that he had a long road of preparation ahead of him. But as for right now, the only thing that he needed was a good night's sleep.

CHAPTER 9

The next morning was particularly difficult for Damien. Trying to come to grips with his unusual dream proved to be more unnerving than he realized initially - even paralyzing. He was unsure what to make of it. Was it only a dream? Was it the future? Some alternate reality? He didn't know. He had no way of knowing. The only thing that he could be certain of was that something wasn't right, and he had to find out what it was.

After showering, Damien went to the gym to blow off some steam. He started off running, first, to clear his head. He ran mile after mile to get some clarity, but it only raised more questions in his mind. When that didn't work, he went to bench presses. He started with one hundred pounds. That wasn't enough, so he increased it gradually up to two hundred, two hundred fifty, three hundred... but nothing could satisfy his anger and confusion. It consumed him. So much so, that he eventually began to sweat blood.

When he finally finished his workout, Damien decided that the exercise wasn't enough. So, he gathered his belongings and made his mind up to go to the surface to get some fresh air and blow off a little steam by walking around. At first, he thought about trying to talk his thoughts and feelings through with Christian, thinking that, perhaps, he could somehow reason with him and come up with a logical explanation as to what was happening to him. But he swiftly abandoned that idea. In the end, he decided to go on his own and do his best to figure it out. When he reached the surface, he stood and took a deep breath, put on his headphones, and walked away.

At that moment, Damien held the weight of the entire world on his shoulders. Anxious, he drifted along searching within himself thinking that he would find a deeper meaning to his dreams. Was it only a dream? Could it be some sort of sign, a premonition perhaps? He couldn't be sure. The only thing he found at the end of his introspection was empty thoughts and more questions with no answers. Not ready to retreat to the bunker, he decided to keep moving.

As he walked through the neighborhood, he couldn't help but notice the state of the people that were left on the streets. Most were lined up along the roads in dirty, tattered clothes and looked hungry, tired, and desperate. So many were starving - some to the point of near death. It broke Damien's heart to see the world that he once knew was so far gone, so far from recovery. There were so many buildings along the way with broken windows and kicked-in doors from the masses looting. The world around him had fallen apart and, deep down, Damien knew that it had to change.

By the time he made it back to the base, it was almost dark. So rather than just hang out outside some more, he went inside. Damien decided to make his way to the infirmary in the hope that he could talk to someone about what he was going through. When he got there, he found a doctor - the same one that treated him when he was in his coma.

"Excuse me, doc," he said. "I was wondering if you had someone in that I could talk to?"

"Damien," she said a bit flustered. "It's good to see you again." She sat her bags down and sat down at her desk. "Please, just call me Nadia. Now, tell me exactly what is it that's going on with you?"

Damien sat down and let out a deep sigh.

"What isn't going on? I think I'm losing my mind. Last night, I had the craziest dream. But it felt so real."

"I'm not a dream specialist or anything like that. But I'll try my best to help. What happened in this dream?" Nadia asked.

"I woke up in my dream and everyone here was dead... except for me. I couldn't believe it. I fought a night-stalker inside the cafeteria. Cyris was dead in the training room. Diamond died in my arms trying to warn me. I buried my best friend after that. Then, I managed to make my way up to the surface. But I was blindsided, knocked out, and then helpless as some weird guy in all black held me in the air by my neck and finally killed me. That's when I woke up. Now, the really crazy thing is that, even at this moment, as I'm sure I live and breathe, I just can't come to terms with it being just a dream. I can't! It was too real."

"What made it so real for you?"

"Everything, doc. And I mean everything! The death, the emotions that I felt, facing my own mortality in such a helpless situation. It felt like that day all over again. But I swear, nothing was more real than the man in black. Absolutely nothing."

"Can you describe him?"

"He was... menacing. Just frightening. And that's the strange part about it because nothing scares me. But he did! There wasn't a thing that I could do to stop him. He had me right outside in the middle of the street by my neck as he stabbed my gut with his hand." Damien paused for a moment. "His eyes," he whispered.

"He had these glowing, red eyes underneath the hood of his long, black coat. Almost pulsing. And his voice, it was the stuff of nightmares, Nadia..."

Nadia took a moment to gather her thoughts and as she glanced at Damien, she had a look of complete worry and nervousness on her face.

"Damien, how much do you know about the day the Event took place? Any specific details about what happened come to mind?"

"Nothing specific," Damien answered. "Just what happened with my family mostly. Why?"

Nadia appeared worried. She was troubled and it showed.

"So, you've never heard about what specifically happened at Ground Zero outside of the University of Chicago, Damien?"

"No, no deep, intricate details. I only just found out that Cyris was the one who led the assault at Ground Zero. What would that have to do with my dream?"

"I really think that you should talk to him. I think he might be able to help you more – a lot more than I can with this. And trust me, no physical doctor or psych doctor can help you with this situation. It's more delicate than you think."

Damien agreed. But he was more puzzled now than he was before he walked in. There were so many thoughts that clouded his mind that he couldn't find a way to sort through them all. It felt to him like a dense fog that shadowed his entire essence. But none of that changed the fact that he was desperate for answers.

Nadia went into her office, picked up the phone, and called Cyris. After a brief conversation, she expressed that Damien had something to discuss with him. "It's important," she stressed. So, within a matter of minutes, he arrived at the clinic.

"What's going on, Nadia?" Cyris asked.

"It's Damien. He's obviously has been through it with the coma and taking on the Night-stalkers, and he's expected to have some sort of trauma or PTSD, but what he just told me, Cyris... he's having more than just bad dreams."

"You did right to call me," he said. "I'll take it from here. Thank you." Cyris walked over to Damien.

"What's going on, son? Nadia tells me that you're having some sort of bad dream?"

Damien explained the dream to Cyris. He listened intently as certain details came to light. By the time he was finished, Cyris couldn't believe what he had heard. Everything appeared as a simple dream up until Damien described the mysterious man. The description of the man in black was spot on to what Cyris had experienced during the Event. It was enough to send chills down his spine right down to the marrow of his bones.

"Damien," Cyris said, "Come with me." He looked over at Nadia and shook her hand. "Thank you, Nadia. We'll be in touch."

Cyris and Damien left the infirmary and headed to the training room. The walk there was a silent one. Damien wondered what all of this meant. Why was this happening to him? What was he seeing? More importantly, though, who was he seeing? It left him puzzled. And there weren't any answers coming fast enough.

As they arrived at the training room, they walked over to one of the benches and sat down.

"Damien, I think I'm beginning to understand what's going on with you," Cyris said. "I suspected something yesterday when we were training. The way you moved... the ferocity in your combat, the speed, agility; everything seemed different from when you fought the Night-stalkers at the mall."

Damien looked confused. He didn't quite understand.

"I want you to listen very closely to what I'm going to tell you, Damien. When the Event started, I was in command of the unit sent to investigate Ground Zero. It started as just what seemed to be an electrical storm We all thought it was a small electrical storm in the middle of the street. But at the same time, it was a bit suspicious. I had my tech officer run diagnostics on the area after a hole just opened up right in front of us. I swear, we couldn't believe it. The crowd in front of the university just watched and waited. When it was decided that the hole wasn't just a hole, that it was a gateway - some kind of portal - we tried to close it. I promise you, Damien, we tried our best. But we couldn't."

At this point, Cyris was fighting back tears, but he couldn't hold down his emotions. "It was pointless. Minutes later, the Night-stalkers came through and ripped through my squad. Then, within a matter of minutes, their attention was on the rest of the planet. The people watching were instant victims. Every one of them was slaughtered like cattle, and we couldn't do anything but watch in complete horror. It was a massacre. I still have nightmares about it to this day."

"During the fighting, both myself and my science officer were knocked back by a huge blast. Private David Smith. He died upon impact. I was knocked unconscious but, somehow, I managed to survive. Maybe it was to finally tell this tale. But when I woke up, Damien, there was a man standing above me... a man with a long, black, hooded coat standing next to me. His voice was terrifying. His exact words were, 'You couldn't stop this, Collins. You don't have the power to stop me. And you'd be foolish to think that you could stop what's to come.' And then he told me that the end of our world had begun as he continued to rain down destruction everywhere. And I just laid there on the ground, weak, pathetic, and just waiting to die myself at that point."

"So, after hearing your dream, I can tell you with certainty that the person that you saw is, in fact, very real and very terrifying. And Damien, I don't know how it's possible or what exactly is your connection to him, but I think your fight with the Night-stalkers may have unlocked or even unleashed something inside of you and you're more important than we may have all realized. But I promise you, Damien, you're not going crazy and we'll figure it out. And we'll do it together. Remember, you're one of us now."

With that small amount of reassurance, Damien got up to leave. Just before he made it to the door Nadia stopped him.

"Are you alright?" she asked. "Did talking to Cyris help at all."

He paused. "It helped a little. It gave me some insight. But I honestly have more questions now than I did before. Who is this guy? If I've never seen him in person, then why is he showing up in my dreams? Is there a purpose to all of this? It's just got me confused."

Nadia took his hand. "It is confusing. Probably scary, too. But if you need a friend, someone to talk to, or anything at all, I'm here."

Damien smiled back at Nadia and left the room still uncertain about anything. The only thing that he knew was that his dreams were only the beginning.

CHAPTER 10

Another night passed and it proved to be a difficult one for Damien. Not only were the nightmares worse than the night before, but this time, he woke up with extreme heat radiating from his body. He didn't feel sick or feverish or anything of that nature. He was only hot.

As he got out of bed, he went over to the thermostat to check the temperature and his room was at a moderate seventy-two degrees. Thinking that maybe it was broken, he hit it a few times to see if it would glitch, and when that did nothing, he walked to the vent to check it but there wasn't any type of air coming out of it. Thinking that just maybe he was imagining things, he went on about his normal morning routine. So, after his training session with Cyris, he went to meet Christian down in the hangar.

Meanwhile, Christian was prepping his truck for the day. He took the time to empty anything unnecessary for the trip and even planned for Jimmy to join him.

"Come on, Jimmy," Christian shouted. "We need to move fast if we're gonna be back by sundown."

Jimmy did the best he could to get his bag ready for his trip with Christian. They were going on a supply run and Christian wanted to make good time and be back before sunset because that's when the danger was the worst, and the Night-stalkers ran the streets.

As they got in the truck, Damien ran up to them.

"You guys are finally making that run?" he asked.

"Yeah, we're headed back out south today towards Homewood," Christian answered. "Food, electronics... the usual stuff. I think we need some building tools, too. I'm not sure."

"Yeah, Christian is gonna show me how to take some parts off of some old computers! I can't wait!" Jimmy was very enthusiastic. It was the first time since being in the bunker that he got to spend any time with Christian or Damien. So, he was very excited.

Damien laughed. "Oh, is he?" he said jokingly. He looked over at Christian. "Be careful, Chris, seriously. Take care of him. It's really bad out there right now and I have a bad feeling."

Christian got in the truck and started the ignition and soon after, Jimmy followed. "Oh, Damien. I didn't know you cared so much," Christian joked.

"I don't," he quipped. "But who else is gonna laugh at my bad jokes? Just be safe..."

As Damien walked away, Christian and Jimmy drove off.

When they got outside, everything looked clear. There was no sign of danger on the street or anywhere in the vicinity. So, they headed out on their mission to obtain supplies. As they drove off, Christian pulled out a CD and put it on the radio. Jimmy looked over at Christian.

"What is that you just put on?" Jimmy asked.

"Linkin Park's second album - Meteora," Christian answered. "This was one of my favorite CDs when I was a kid."

"Who is Linkin Park?"

"Aw, Jimmy, have I got some things to teach you..." So, Christian turned up the radio and kept driving.

"So, where are we going anyway?" Jimmy asked.

"To this area where there was a grocery store, hardware store, and some other things that we need. There's a huge electronics store over that way, too, that used to sell computer parts and whole computer systems and software. We couldn't get any of it the last time when we were at the mall because of what happened. So, maybe this time, we can gather what we need and get back."

"Do you think it's safe?"

"I sure hope so, Jimmy. We need these supplies. The Pack needs these supplies."

After a lengthy drive, they finally arrived at Washington Square. As they pulled up, all seemed quiet. Christian got out of the truck, very hesitantly, because he knew things could go south very quickly. Once Christian gave Jimmy the all-clear, he got out of the truck, too.

As they made their way through the door of an old Home Depot store, a loud wind could be heard throughout the building. It was the sound of emptiness and desolation. Very eerie. They stopped from aisle to aisle to recover any items that they could. Drills and hand tools, lumber and sheet metal, and cleaning supplies; any and everything was fair game. And they did their best not to leave anything out.

When they finally reached the electronics store, a Best Buy store that was across the street, everything was in disarray. It was a clear example of the devastation left behind after the Event. Monitors had been smashed, and hard drives and motherboards were scattered throughout the store. It was a complete mess from the riots and looting that took place afterward.

"Alright, Jimmy," Christian said, "We'll start with the computer parts and any monitors that we can salvage. Then we'll look for cables and software."

The two of them went through almost every computer and component that was laying around the store that seemed useable. Little by little, they took monitors, computer towers, graphics cards, two-way radios, cell phones, and the like. A lot of these were supplies that had been missing at the bunker for some time now or were on their last leg. This was a much-needed victory for The Pack as a whole.

When everything was gathered, they began moving everything outside. All seemed to be quiet, but Christian took every precaution that he could think of anyway. By the time that they finished, the sun had begun to set as they had spent several hours there. Christian knew that it could get dangerous fast and, this time, there was no Damien or anyone else around to protect them.

After loading the last of the supplies onto the truck, the two got inside and raced off to beat the sun. As they drove, Christian had a strange feeling in the pit of his stomach. It was almost as if he knew something was wrong. It made him feel uneasy, nauseous even. He looked into the sky and noticed that the clouds were darker than usual. Thunder rumbled across the sky and lightning strikes started to follow soon after.

Suddenly, as they approached the bunker, a violent storm broke out, and the rain fell hard enough to shatter the windshield of the truck. Christian began to drive faster until he noticed several strange noises. Jimmy sat in the passenger seat terrified, gripping it tightly, at the strength of the storm and the sounds that were surrounding them. Suddenly, Christian slammed on the brakes as hard as he could at the sight of several Night-stalkers in the middle of the street. He swerved to get out of the way, but the slippery road and the sudden jerk made the truck roll over to the side of the road and smash into a building a few blocks away from the hideout.

Christian looked over at Jimmy. Both were barely conscious. He looked around after that and realized that the truck itself was upside down. Christian pulled out a knife and struggled to cut himself free. As he fell to the top of the truck, things started to look worse. The accident caused the truck to ignite from gas leaking and the surrounding flames. Knowing that the Night-stalkers were still out there and possibly closing in on them, Christian tried to free an unconscious Jimmy from his seat belt, but it proved more difficult than he could have predicted. Time wasn't on his side, and as the flames increased, Christian finally freed Jimmy, but not before a Night-stalker reached in and grabbed Jimmy by the leg. In a panic, Christian quickly stabbed the creature in the hand, and it released its grip. Just as Christian pulled Jimmy out of the truck it exploded and sent them both flying into the wall of the building nearby.

Christian got up and picked Jimmy up but struggled to walk away as his leg and back were injured from the blast. As the storm got more violent the sky darkened to pitch black. Multiple lightning bolts could be seen stretched across the sky as black clouds soared over them. Christian, barely conscious himself, fell to his knees still holding Jimmy. In the distance, he heard several motorcycles approaching at a quick pace. The sound of rapid gunfire filled the air along with the howls and growls of the Night-stalkers.

"Christian! Christian, can you hear me?!" It was Damien calling out. "Chris! Where could he be?" he thought to himself.

He stopped and looked around and noticed the carnage and the wreckage and ran towards it. When he got over near the truck, he saw both Christian and Jimmy lying unconscious. He rushed over to them praying that they were still alive. After checking their pulses, he did the best he could to wake Christian up but was unsuccessful. He reached into his bag and pulled out a syringe with epinephrine. Once he injected Christian with it, he woke up at once.

"We've gotta move, bro," Christian shouted.

"You don't say???" Damien said sarcastically. "Let's MOVE!" Christian ran off as Damien picked up Jimmy and ran behind him.

Just then, a truck pulled up with Cyris behind the wheel and Diamond in the passenger seat. Damien went to put Jimmy in the back of the truck and Christian got in afterward. Immediately, Damien ran back off to fight the remaining creatures. Cyris and Diamond, without hesitation, got out of the truck, grabbed their weapons, and joined the fight.

All three of them fought furiously to take down creature after creature. The more that they killed the more that kept coming and things quickly became overwhelming. The soldiers that they brought with them fell easily one by one until no one was left but them. Just as Diamond was about to call a retreat...

"ENOUGH!" a menacing voice announced from a nearby rooftop. Damien, Diamond, and Cyris all looked up and saw a shadowy figure standing tall on the roof. He was hooded with a long, black coat blowing in the wind. Under the hood, no face could be seen. Only a slight red glow around the eyes.

"I can't believe it," Cyris said. "It's him."

"Him?" Diamond questioned. "Him who? It can't be...."

The man then jumped to the ground from the rooftop with ease and disappeared into the darkness.

"I'm here," he said from behind them as he knocked down both Cyris and Diamond. He then grabbed Damien by the neck and hoisted him up in the air with one hand and removed his hood with the other.

What was underneath shocked Damien to his core. It was a skull-shaped mask with glowing red eyes underneath. Gradually, the glow dissipated, and only brown eyes could be seen behind the mask as he looked into Damien's eyes.

"Hello, Damien," he said. "Allow me to introduce myself. My name is Dante."

Damien struggled to speak. "I don't care who you are."

"Oh, but you will, Damien. You will, indeed." He looked Damien up and down. "You're not quite ready yet. No. Definitely, not ready."

"Ready for what?!"

"You will see Damien. Yes, you will. But for now, you'll just have to wait."

"I'll KILL you!"

"Not yet. For now, I let you go. But I'll tell you what I told your friend two years ago... Everything you know is ending. You can't stop it, Damien." Dante dropped Damien to the ground and Damien took a moment to catch his breath. By the time he looked up, Dante was gone.

Once Damien regained his breath, he woke Diamond and Cyris up. As they regained full consciousness, Damien stood in the middle of the road looking at the rooftops to see if he could spot Dante. But all of his attempts were unsuccessful, and the skies finally had begun to clear up.

"Damien," Diamond shouted. "You alright?"

"No," he answered in frustration. "I'm far from it."

"Come on," Cyris said. "We still have to get these two back to the bunker."

So, Damien got on his motorcycle and drove off while Cyris and Diamond took off in the truck. Now that they finally knew who they were up against, the real challenge now lay in preparing to take him down. But for someone so strong and so fast, was any amount of training going to be enough? Only time would tell now...

CHAPTER 11

T he next day at the station, Damien was having a difficult time processing his encounter with Dante. The strength that Dante had, the speed, agility, and knowledge that he had overwhelmed Damien to the point where he couldn't sleep or eat. Perhaps, the most important question was how did Dante know who Damien was? How could he know anyone if he was from another world? What did he mean when he said that Damien wasn't ready? And ready for what exactly? But indeed, the answers he looked for, he knew, would have to wait. The more pressing matter at hand was figuring out where Dante was and how could they stop him.

For most of the day, Damien spent his time in the training room. For him, not only was this a time for him to get in peak physical condition, but it was also a time to gather his thoughts and figure out his next move. He knew that he couldn't be rash and act impulsively. He would need to act more as if he was playing a game of chess and actively plot his course of action with Diamond, Cyris, and Christian.

"Hi, Damien," Nadia said as she walked in. "How are you?"

"Dr. Montgomery, I'm alright, I guess," he said. "Just trying to blow off a little bit of steam."

"Please, call me Nadia. Do you mind if I join you?"

"Sure."

So, she sat down next to Damien and began her exercise routine. The silence and tension between them couldn't be more awkward.

"So..." Damien started.

"I heard..." Nadia interrupted.

They both laughed it off. And then Damien spoke.

"Please," he said, "You go first."

"I heard about yesterday's encounter," she said.

Damien took a deep breath and let out a huge sigh.

"Yeah. Yeah, yesterday was very interesting. It was a disaster. The guy from my dream... it was him. It was really him. I couldn't believe it. And he was so fast... and strong."

Nadia looked very concerned at Damien. "Is that why you've been here all night and morning killing yourself in this gym?"

"How did you know I was here all night?"

"I stopped by your room last night after I heard about what happened. I was coming to check on you."

Damien got up from the bench press and wiped the sweat off of him.

"Look, Nadia," Damien said. "I'm going to go to the surface in a little bit. I've gotta do some investigating. All of this has been sitting on my mind pretty heavily. I could really use the company... and an extra set of eyes. That is if you're up to it."

Nadia couldn't help but blush. She smiled as she got up from the exercise bike.

"Damien, are you asking me on a date?"

He laughed it off but was clearly embarrassed. "I don't know if this would exactly qualify as a date. But I would appreciate your presence. I feel pretty comfortable with you and being around you."

"I would love to join you, Damien," Nadia said.

"Great! Meet me in the hangar in about forty-five minutes."

Nadia quickly agreed and they parted ways. Damien was more nervous than he cared to admit. He liked Nadia a lot but his fear of losing someone close to him again was more paralyzing than he could've ever imagined. But what could he do? He knew that he couldn't pass this up. He had to make a move.

Damien's mind pulled him in different directions. On one hand, he thought about what his time coming up with Nadia could mean for both of them. Could he possibly find love in this crazy world filled with pain and despair? But on the other hand, there was Dante. Damien knew that he was still out there and that he had a long way to go before he could face him. He wasn't strong enough and he knew it. How could he overcome that? Could he?

Just as he was about to head out of the door of his room there was a knock at the door. It was Christian and Diamond.

"Hey, I'm about to head to the surface so..."

"D, this won't take long, bro," Christian said.

"Look," Diamond started. "We've been doing some thinking. We suspected this after you first woke up. But in recent days, with your increased strength, speed, and agility, your dream the other night, and your encounter with Dante last night..."

"You're more connected to the bigger picture, Damien, than any of us ever knew," Christian finished. "I mean, when you found me, I was almost dead. Buried under that rubble. But you got me out. You mustered every bit of strength that you had and pulled me out when I had given up. I was near death, and you brought me back. I always knew in my heart that you were special."

"So now, Damien, we're going to get to the root of it all," Diamond said.

"That's good," Damien said. "Thank you. I've got a little bit of digging to do myself. As a matter of fact, that's actually what I'm going to do now."

"Where are you going to look?" Christian asked.

"I need to go back to where it all started. Not just for me... for everyone. I need answers."

Diamond stepped in. "Do you need a team to go with you?"

"Nah, I'm good," Damien said. "I have someone riding with me. Keep digging. See what you can find. We'll trade notes when I get back."

Everyone agreed and they all exited the room.

When Damien got to the hangar, he walked over to his motorcycle. He stood for a few minutes and waited for Nadia to get there. Just as he got ready to get on the bike and leave, Nadia entered the hangar. Her beauty struck Damien hard. He couldn't believe how beautiful she was but, of course, he had to keep his composure.

"I am so sorry that I'm so late," Nadia said. "I had an issue at the clinic."

"Everything cool?"

"Yeah, we're good. Let's ride."

With that, they both got on the motorcycle and left.

As they rode through the city, they couldn't help but see all of the people living on the streets that were affected by the invasion. In his heart, Damien knew that it wasn't right. The sight of the pain of the people enraged him. He felt a sense of duty to help to put the lives of the innocent back together. To make things right, he knew that he would, no doubt, go to any length.

Nadia, for her part, felt extreme sadness for everyone. The people living on the streets, where it wasn't safe to be day or night, moved her to tears. For comfort, she wrapped her arms around Damien tighter as she kept weeping and they continued riding through the city.

Finally, they reached Ground Zero – the UIC Campus on Taylor and Halsted St. - the place where it all started. The tanks and trucks that were there on that fateful day remained in place – weathered and rusted – just the same as the day everything happened. The carnage there was truly unbelievable. Skeletons were scattered throughout the area. The two of them looked in horror as they finally got a grasp on the devastation left behind after the Event as this was their first time visiting the site.

"Nadia, don't go off too far. It's still not too safe." She agreed as they both began to investigate. Damien stopped and pulled out a small device from his backpack and turned it on. "OK. So, from what I understand from that day, they all came through some kind of portal right over the other side of the street or right in middle across from the campus grounds. I'm not totally sure."

"Yeah, that's what I heard about it, too," Nadia said. "So, I guess that's the direction we need to head in."

"Agreed." Damien reached into his backpack and pulled out a nine-millimeter handgun and gave it to Nadia. "You ever used one of these before?"

"Maybe twice," Nadia said as she took the gun from him. "I can handle it. Don't worry."

As they walked toward the road, they moved with extreme caution. Damien pulled a small device out of his pocket.

"What's that?" Nadia asked.

"It's something Christian put together for me last night after our little encounter with Dante. It picks up traces of any rifts in space and time."

As they walked, the device beeped showing the location of the original rift. As they got closer, the beeps became more erratic. Very soon, they came upon the spot.

"We got it, Nadia. Reach in my bag and pull out the temporal displacement monitor."

Once they got the monitor set up, they both sat down next to each other in the grass and waited as the machine did its job. An awkward silence filled the space between the two of them as they waited. Each of them knew that they wanted to say something to the other but felt that the mission was more important.

"What do you think is on the other side?" Nadia asked.

"Who knows? It could be anything. If it's anything like the movies back in the day showed, it could be a mirror image of this world, it could be an entirely different planet. All I know is I need to find out. There are too many questions that don't have answers."

Nadia reached for Damien's hand, grabbed it, and held on as tightly as she could.

"I really hope we find those answers," she said.

Damien looked at Nadia and held her close.

After twenty minutes, the monitor started beeping.

"Great!" Damien said. "Let's pack this stuff up. We got what we need. Come on. There's one more place I wanna go before we head back."

As they packed everything away, Nadia reached over to grab Damien and she gave him a big - yet unexpected - kiss. Damien couldn't believe it. She made the first move, and he was shocked just as much as he wanted it to happen. He looked up at her and smiled.

"What was that for?" he asked.

Nadia broke down into tears.

"Damien, I've lost so much to this war. My mom, my brother, my home: the past couple of years have been rough. When everything happened, I was with someone. He was my first love. My only love. This war took him away... right in front of me. After that, I knew in my heart that I would never fall in love again. But then you came along. I took care of you while you were in the coma. I was told about how you saved your friends and all those children. Christian told me stories about how you took care of him for the past two years. I just knew you were special. I knew you without even speaking to you. I fell in love with you then. And then last night happened. You threw yourself in harm's way without even questioning it. I want you to know that through all of this, you have someone to come back to. Someone who's not afraid to love you. And I know that you may not feel the same way about me, but it doesn't matter. I love you and I'm never leaving your side, Damien. Life is too short, and I want to be the one that you can come to in the best and worst of times. I love you."

Damien, at a loss for words, just grabbed Nadia and kissed her passionately.

"Come on. Let's get out of here," he told her as he took her hand.

They picked everything up, got on the motorcycle, and drove away. As they drove through the city, they welcomed the fresh air and nice weather. They also enjoyed the bliss of their newfound love for each other, but at the same time, they knew more work needed to be done. Romance would have to wait.

They eventually pulled up in front of an old abandoned house. As they got off the motorcycle, Damien looked up at the ruins of the house. Nadia looked around to survey the area.

"I know this neighborhood," she said.

"It's the Marycrest subdivision of Country Club Hills," Damien answered. He walked up to the front door. "This was my home. Come on."

As they walked inside, memories started coming back for Damien. He remembered all of the years he spent in this house growing up. The love that his parents had for him, and his sister was unforgettable. Damien grabbed Nadia's hand as they traversed through the rubble. Beams and drywall from the ceiling had fallen to the floor and scorch marks were all over the walls and floor.

When they walked into the kitchen, the damage there wasn't as bad. They walked over to the cabinet and Damien pulled down his father's favorite coffee mug. It was still intact even after these two years. He wrapped it up with one of the random dish towels on the counter and put it in his bag. As he opened the refrigerator, the smell of rotten food permeated the air leaving a foul stench worse than death. Immediately, he closed it up and walked away.

They eventually left the kitchen to head upstairs. The first place they went was to his parents' bedroom. He sat on their bed and started to weep.

"They should've been here, Nadia. They should've made it out."

"How did they die... if you don't mind me asking?"

"Trying to save me," he said as he got up and walked out of the bedroom.

Nadia quickly followed.

"I'm sorry, Damien. I didn't mean to upset you."

"It's cool. Don't sweat it. I'm good..."

They walked over to the next room to get to Damien's bedroom. Damien paused as he took a deep breath and they started to walk into the room. They opened the door slowly. When they got in, what they found was unbelievable. Someone sitting in Damien's chair. The man stood up.

"Hello, Damien," he said as he turned around.

"DANTE!" Damien yelled out.

Damien quickly rushed him to the ground at lightning speed. Nadia couldn't believe how fast he moved. She had never seen anything like it.

"What are you doing here?"

"Relax, Damien. I didn't come here to fight you. At least, not today. I only came to talk."

"Give me one good reason why I shouldn't snap your neck right now."

Dante grabbed Damien and threw him to the wall. Nadia quickly rushed to Damien's side as Dante got up.

"As I said, Damien, I didn't come for a fight. You and I need to talk."

Damien stood up and brushed himself off.

"You and I have absolutely nothing to talk about," Damien exclaimed. The anger in his eyes began to show. "There's nothing that you could say in this world or the next that would make me want to hear anything you have to say."

"Oh, what I could tell you about worlds," Dante started. "But not today. Listen, you want to get stronger, Damien, but don't know how. You want to end the suffering on your world, but you have no clue how to stop me. Damien, your fight - your entire war - is pointless. My Night-stalkers will rip through your people like the plague and wipe out your entire existence. And all you can do is just stand by and watch. This world is already dead, Damien. There's nothing you can do about it."

"Why are you here?! You destroyed our world, decimated nearly the entire human race, and forced us all into hiding. For what? What was it for? To watch us suffer? What did you mean last night when you said that I wasn't ready? Ready for what? What is the point of all this? What's the point in you just popping up and speaking in riddles? What do you want from me?!"

"Oh, Damien, Damien, Damien," Dante started. "You remind me so much of myself. The anger, the rage... will you channel it, or will you let it all consume you? You see, Damien, there's a force inside of you just screaming out to you to be awakened. But you haven't heard its voice. Listen to your inner voice and channel your fire, your lightning, your rage. Become one with yourself. Only then will you be ready to face me. Don't concern yourself as to why I'm here, boy. Awaken yourself and see the fire and lightning. Then you will have your answers that you seek so diligently and not a second sooner."

"I will stop you, Dante. You have my word."

Dante walked toward the door to leave, but not before he stopped and looked at Damien.

"Perhaps, you will, Damien," Dante said. "Perhaps, indeed. But not before I have everything and everyone you love fallen to their knees and suffer my wrath. In the end, you will stand alone." With that, Dante walked out of the room and completely vanished leaving Damien and Nadia to contemplate not only their futures but the fate of the entire planet.

CHAPTER 12

Damien called for the nearest guard when he and Nadia returned to the base. The anger in his eyes was very clear. The nerve he felt that Dante had to show up at his home as if they were friends didn't sit right with him. At that point, Damien was now a man on a very clear mission: putting an end to Dante and his reign of terror forever.

When the guard came over, Damien gave him explicit instructions.

"Get this bag over to Christian. Then I need you to get a message to Diamond, Cyris, and Christian to meet me in the main conference room in fifteen minutes. Let them know that it's of the utmost importance."

The guard at once went to carry out his orders. Nadia looked over to Damien and rested her hand on his shoulder to comfort him.

"Are you okay?" she asked.

Damien turned and held her close.

"No, babe, I'm not okay. Not one bit. He was at my parents' house sitting in my room. That's just a bit too close to home for me – literally." Damien started pacing back and forth furiously until he finally rested and banged his hand against his motorcycle. "I don't get it. Why me? What does he want from me?"

"I don't know," she answered. "But I know for a fact that you're not alone. You've got Christian, Cyris, and Diamond, and you have me. You'll figure this out - all of you will. Let's just pray that we figure it out before he decides to make his next move."

"I think that may not be too far ahead of us," Damien said. "I'm just worried that whatever he has planned could mean the end for everyone and somehow it's gonna all be my fault."

"Whatever happens is on him, Damien. Not you," Nadia reassured him. "Always remember that." Nadia kissed him softly and held his hand. "Go take care of what you need to take care of. I need to stop by the clinic for a while. I'll come by and check on you later."

Damien agreed and they parted ways.

When he finally reached his room, Damien put up his weapons and lay on his bed to gather his thoughts. For him, everything seemed to be happening so fast and all at once. Just a few short weeks ago, he and Christian were chasing scraps in abandoned neighborhoods but living peacefully. Never for a second had he imagined that he would be caught in the center of an apparent interdimensional war. His life surely took a drastic turn. He couldn't help but think, also, about his parents. He always wondered if they would be proud of the man that he was becoming - whether he was living up to or could live up to their expectations.

Damien got up to wash his face to cool down. His mind was racing. His latest encounter with Dante weighed heavily on his mind. What could he possibly want? What's the end game? Where does this all lead? His mind was flooded with questions. It was time to find the answers.

A few minutes later, everyone met in the conference room. As everyone sat down, Damien came in last and stood at the head of the table.

"As you all know," Damien started, "last night, we had a major development. We finally came face to face with the enemy - an enemy we now know by the name of Dante. We don't know what his plan is yet but whatever it is, it's become pretty plain to see that whatever it is, I'm at the heart of it."

"How can you be so sure of that?" Diamond asked.

Damien sat down. "Last night when we first met, he spoke to me as if he knew me. And I mean like he knew me personally. He looked me dead in my eyes and told me that I'm not ready to face him."

Christian interrupted, "Maybe he was just trying to get under your skin, bro."

"Yeah, he did that. But then I saw him today, too," Damien said.

"Where?" Cyris asked.

"Home... my old home in Country Club Hills... in my bedroom. He was there waiting for me as if he knew I would be there today."

Everyone sat for a moment in a state of disbelief.

"What did he say to you?" Christian asked.

"He told me that he had just come to talk, and that's just what he did. But it was what he said to me that bothered me," Damien started. "He told me again that I wasn't ready and that I need to awaken something that's inside of me."

Diamond sat in confusion. "Something like what, Damien? What's supposed to be inside of you? What does he expect from you?"

"I really wish that I knew. I honestly just thought that he was speaking in riddles and monologuing like a typical villain. But let's be real, who knows with this guy?" Damien said with a long, depressing sigh. "It's frustrating."

"It may be wise for you to take extreme caution when dealing with him, Damien," Cyris started. "We have no idea who this guy is or what exactly he wants. And the fact that he's so invested in you has me a bit uneasy. I don't like it."

"Neither do I. But whatever it is, I'm sure he didn't cross dimensions or wherever he's from and spend two years terrorizing the world just to have a pow-wow with Damien and air out his grievances," Christian said. "We're missing something, and I bet that it's right in front of our faces."

"Indeed, we are," Diamond said. "What about the data from today? What did you pick up with that?"

"We found the actual ground zero," Damien said. "The absolute point where they crossed over into this world."

"We?" Cyris asked.

"Yeah, Dr. Montgomery came along with me."

"We can talk about that later," Cyris said. "What does the data say?"

Christian looked down at his tablet. "Amazingly, there are still readable electrical signatures present from two years ago," Christian started. "There's a lot that I can use here. But from a preliminary standpoint, I would assume that if we can recreate the same electric charge that created the original breach, and it would have to be a significant charge, we may be able to reopen it, send Dante back to where he came from and close it back up for good."

Diamond looked over at Christian. "How long do you need?"

"With a good team, about a week," Christian said.

"We'll arrange to get you who and what you need," Cyris said. "This meeting is adjourned."

As everyone got up, Cyris and Damien stayed behind.

"What's on your mind, Cyris?"

He got up and walked over to Damien and sat next to him. "We live a dangerous life, son, in a dangerous time. Whenever we walk out of those doors there's a big chance that we may not come back. The things that we face, sometimes they're unthinkable, they're more than we can bear. And we may need someone to understand."

"I get it, Cyris," Damien said. "This life is a risk."

"No, son. It can be so much more than just a risk." Cyris started, "Let me tell you a story. There once was a young man who wanted so badly to save his city from the darkness that it faced. He did a fine job, Damien. But he didn't want to be his city's protector for the rest of his life. He dreamt of living a normal life. A life where he would get married and have children. And he had a woman that was willing to be with him, too. But it was only if he gave up this other life. But he knew he had a mission that he needed to see through. One day, he came upon a new type of enemy - an enemy that he didn't fully understand. An enemy that was sure to push him to his very limits and shake his very foundation. This enemy discovered a way to get to the young man - the woman he so loved. Despite the man's best efforts, however, he couldn't protect the one thing that meant the most to him and he blamed himself for not being able to protect her - his precious love."

"Is that something that you went through?" Damien asked. "Are you the guy?"

"No, I'm not. I never got married even though there was some-one special once," Cyris answered. "It's actually from the movie 'The Dark Knight.' It came out when I was a kid. Great movie," he mused as Damien looked at him confused. "But the point is if you're going to get involved with her, be sure that you can protect her, Damien, in all aspects. Keep her away from this part of your life. Because I guarantee you, if that psychopath out there gets the chance, he will use her against you. And nine times out of ten, you'll have to make a choice that you don't want to make: her life or the mission? Think about it, son."

Cyris got up and walked out. Damien was left in the room contemplating his situation with Nadia and wondering if it was the best idea to get involved with her. He knew that what Cyris said made sense, but at the same time, he knew what his heart wanted and needed. Even though he and Nadia had just started this new phase in their lives, she made him feel alive, and he knew in his heart that she felt the same way. After a few minutes, he got up and walked out.

When Damien reached his room, he called Nadia to come over to his room to keep him company. She arrived about an hour later after spending time down at the clinic. Immediately after she got there, Damien sat her down on the bed and then sat next to her and held her hand tightly.

"Nadia, how do you feel about me?" he asked. "Do you think that we could try this relationship and be happy?"

"What do you mean?"

"Just what I said," he replied. "Do you feel that this could work?"

She took a deep breath. "Honestly, Damien. I'm falling for you. I've been falling ever since I first saw you."

"But why?"

"Damien, what's wrong?" she asked sensing that something was wrong.

"Please, Nadia," Damien said. "Just tell me why."

"I fell for you because I could sense your selflessness. To know that you were willing to sacrifice everything in that one fight to protect a bunch of kids that you've never met speaks volumes about the type of man you are. You're honorable, caring, brave, and loving. It just melted me away, Damien. And that was all before even speaking to you. You asked me if I thought we could make it work. My answer is yes. Absolutely! I wholeheartedly believe that."

"Here's the thing... I don't want you to be in any unnecessary danger because of me. With Dante out there and with him being so fixated on me, it automatically puts you in the line of fire just for being close to me. What if I can't protect you? What then? If he gets to you just to spite me and I can't save you, I wouldn't be able to live with myself, Nadia. I couldn't."

"That's my risk to take, Damien. I knew that the second we kissed. But, babe, every moment could be the last. That fact remains whether we're together or not." She kissed him softly on his cheek while holding his hand. "So why not be together? Let's love each other. Let's take advantage of every moment that we're together and treat it like it could be our last moment. I don't wanna hold back. And I don't want you to either."

"Why don't you stay here tonight?" Damien suggested. "I could really use the company."

"I wouldn't have it any other way," Nadia replied as she kissed him tenderly and caressed his back.

Later that night, as they lay in bed together, a sleepless Damien stared endlessly at the ceiling going over in his mind how fortunate he had been the past few weeks ending up with a new home, friends, and even a new love. He felt good about himself for the first time in over two years.

Conversely, he had a tight knot in the pit of his stomach thinking about the potential consequences of the war with Dante and the Night-stalkers. Even though the risks of getting close weighed on his mind, it was at that moment that he decided that he was going to leap headfirst into love and do all that he could to protect

Nadia. At that moment as she lay snuggled under him with her head on his chest, he knew that she was his priority and their lives would forever be bonded together in love.

Shortly afterward, he leaned over and kissed her on her forehead as she slept. As he reached over to the light off, he noticed it starting to flicker. Thinking nothing of it, he continued to reach for the lamp and, as he touched it, a burst of electricity ran through his body and the light bulb popped exposing the base of the bulb. Frustrated at this latest happening, Damien finally closed his eyes and went to sleep.

CHAPTER 13

The following morning, Damien rolled over, gazed at Nadia as she lay sleeping, and smiled to himself. He was in awe, not only because of her beauty but because he was getting a genuine chance at some kind of happiness in these dark times. Deeper than that, however, he saw this new relationship as a chance to love just as his parents did. That didn't mean, though, that Cyris' words didn't stay pressed upon his mind. As he watched as Nadia lay in bed still sleeping, he questioned if he possessed the strength and will that it would take to protect her from the madness and evil that Dante had unleashed upon the earth.

As Damien got out of bed, Nadia woke up soon after - with a smile no less. She immediately jumped up and pulled him back into bed.

"And where do you think you're going, mister?" Nadia asked playfully.

"Getting ready to go help Chris and Diamond with the portal device."

"Come back to bed."

Damien smiled and kissed her. "Oh, I wish. But I promised them that I would come to the lab and help with this device, and you need to get to the clinic. We'll have time to hang out later. I promise. But we need to get on the move, babe." He leaned over to give her another kiss.

Nadia wasn't happy but she knew in her heart that he was right. "God, you just have to make sense? Don't you?" She sat up. "OK, I'll tell you what... We can meet for lunch around 1:00. That sound good?"

"It's a date. I wouldn't miss it."

With that, Damien got in the shower, got dressed, grabbed his bag, and left the room for the laboratory.

As he walked through the halls, Damien had an uneasiness about him. To him, something didn't feel right and he knew it. His stomach started to churn uncontrollably and he ran for the nearest restroom. Once he got to the toilet, he bent over and vomited.

"What is happening to me?" he thought to himself. Damien took a moment to regain his composure but he still felt unsettled. He leaned over the toilet bowl to vomit once again. Only this time, there was a small amount of blood present. Damien sat on the restroom floor next to the toilet and rested with his eyes closed as he started to develop a migraine. His head throbbed unrelentingly as he sat and tried to regain his composure. After about ten minutes of sitting, he decided to get up and keep pushing. So, he washed his hands, left the restroom, and then he was off once again.

As Damien approached the development lab, he could see Christian heading into the lab. He started to jog to meet Christian at the door when, all of a sudden, he had an intense feeling of vertigo and collapsed to the floor. Christian rushed to his aid as fast as he could. By the time he reached Damien, he was unconscious and unresponsive.

"Diamond, page Dr. Montgomery to the development lab! Hurry!"

All he could think was "Not again." For the second time in a matter of weeks, Damien lay unconscious... helpless. Again, his best friend - his brother - was left in a coma with no clue as to what was wrong.

When Nadia arrived, she couldn't believe what she saw. The initial shock froze her at first but she quickly got herself together to care for Damien.

She looked over to Christian. "What happened?"

"I don't know," he answered. "He was jogging towards me and just passed out."

"Just passed out? That's it?" Nadia asked.

"That's it," Christian responded. "He was running my way coming to the lab. The next thing I know, he's hitting the floor."

Nadia started to examine Damien right away looking for any injuries or signs of trauma. "OK. So, I don't see anything visible. No wounds or bleeding of any kind. We need to get him back to the clinic. I wanna run a CT on his head and make sure that there isn't any damage that we may have missed from before." As Nadia reached in to feel his forehead, she could feel an intense heat coming from his body. She touched his arm with the back of her hand and drew back quickly. When she turned her hand over to look at it, she saw that her palm had turned red from the heat. His skin felt as if he was on fire and no one could touch him.

"Christian, get some ice-cold towels," Nadia said. "Grab one of the digital thermometers, too."

"Is there anything that I can do?" Diamond asked.

"Just get that device working," she said. "Whatever is happening with Damien, I'm almost certain that Dante is behind it or is connected in some way. Get it working... Please, Diamond... I can't lose him."

"You won't, Nadia," Diamond reassured her. "He'll make it."

As Christian came back with the towels, Damien began to stir. When he opened his eyes, the first person he saw was Nadia and a big smile came to his face.

"Hey, what happened?" he asked. "Why are we in the hallway?"

Nadia started to shed tears. "I thought I had lost you for a minute."

Damien sat up and kissed her. "Lost me? You can't lose me. You're stuck with me, babe."

"Damien," Christian said, "you need to let Nadia check you out, bro."

Diamond stepped in. "Yeah, Christian and I can handle this."

Damien stood up, stumbling at first. "I'm good... really. Look, I want to help with this. I need to. I need answers just the same as you do."

Nadia looked at him and saw the determination in his eyes. So she said reluctantly, "Fine, Damien. But the second you feel another episode coming on you call me. And not a minute less."

Damien nodded in agreement and went into the lab as Nadia walked away. Once inside, Damien started going through all of the data that he collected on the original breach. Everything looked so cut and dry. Open another wormhole, send Dante and his army back through, and close the breach permanently and that would solve the problem. It all seemed simple enough. But the truth was that Damien knew that nothing was ever all that it seemed to be, and it wouldn't be that simple either.

Overall, Damien seemed to be doing fine physically and he didn't show any other signs of his body overheating or him passing out. But Christian knew deep down that something just wasn't quite right. He felt it in his bones. Damien walked around the lab quiet as a mouse – so focused on the task at hand. He had a clear look on his face of confusion and anguish... determination.

Hours passed in the lab without Damien saying a word. As Christian and Diamond worked together building the breaching device, they knew something was wrong with him, but Damien being the person that he was, didn't want to talk about it. Instead, he chose to focus completely on his work. After a while, he picked up his bag and left to meet Nadia for lunch as they had planned.

As he walked through the complex, Damien could only focus on what was going on with him; the levitation in his sleep, the nightmares, the fainting. It bothered him to no end. To have all of these questions with no possible answer in sight frustrated him. He knew that these things that were happening to him were only the beginning; perhaps, a foreshadowing of things to come.

Damien started walking through the cafeteria aimlessly - in a daze of sorts. Everything to him seemed almost surreal. His vision was thrown off by the bright lights and his body felt extremely fatigued. As he started to stumble through the cafeteria, everyone began to stare at him. His eyes closed and just as he fell to the ground, Nadia ran up to him, caught him, and laid him down. Again, his skin was burning hotter than it was that morning with one major difference this time: he appeared to have a faint, white glow surrounding his entire body.

Nadia stepped back right away to avoid the intensity of the heat coming from him. At this point, she was completely unsure of how to help him. Damien - her heart and her love - just laid there helpless in clear pain. How could she end his suffering? In what way could she help?

Christian and Cyris ran up to Damien to try to assist. Christian quickly pulled Nadia to the side and sat her down to comfort her.

As he did that, Cyris soaked some towels in ice-cold water and brought them over to place on Damien. As soon as he sat them down, the towels began to steam heavily until they eventually caught fire. Right away, Cyris threw the towels off of him to the floor. Seeing that this was more serious than they thought, Christian, then, asked everyone to leave the cafeteria.

"Earlier, Christian, when he passed out, how long did it take for him to recover?" Cyris asked.

"I'd have to say it was about ten minutes, maybe. It wasn't long." Christian looked over to Nadia. "How long has he been out this time?"

"About the same. Maybe ten minutes," she said as she wiped the tears from her face.

"OK," Cyris said. "We need to get him to the clinic somehow."

Cyris reached in to check if Damien had cooled down. As he got closer, Christian looked over at them and noticed something strange... "Cyris, wait! Don't touch him!"

But just as he said that Cyris touched Damien and a huge electrical surge flowed throughout the complex and through Damien and it shocked Cyris so badly that it blew him back into the wall. Nadia and Christian couldn't believe what they had just witnessed. At first, Damien was burning. But now, he's shocking people to the point of near electrocution and propelling them away from him. Cyris, as he recovered, couldn't believe what had happened either. He sat on the wall trying to regain himself but sat in awe at the sheer power coming from Damien.

Soon after, as Cyris got up, Damien got up also.

"What happened?" he asked.

Cyris walked over to him and helped him up. "Damien, we don't know. You passed out again. We were hoping that you could tell us. It was much more serious this time."

Nadia ran to Damien in tears and hugged him tightly. "Damien, we have to find out what's going on."

Damien through all of the chaos just stood there, however, seemingly unphased. "I'm alright, guys. Really. I feel good. I feel better now. Better than I've felt in a while."

Christian stepped in. "Then, how do you explain these episodes, bro? You're not alright. Nothing is at this point."

Damien didn't have an answer. He didn't even know where to start. He just stood there, still and motionless.

Diamond, then, contacted Christian over the radio. "Christian, we've got something. You need to hurry back, NOW!"

Everyone ran to the lab as quickly as possible. When they got there, electricity was surging throughout the room. No one knew what to make of it. Within a few seconds, the electricity started to get more violent and wild. Then suddenly, a big lightning bolt came from Diamond's workstation and fired toward Nadia.

Everything in the room slowed down to a crawl for Damien - almost as if the world around him was going in slow motion. He was clearly focused. He saw that Nadia was in danger and he raced toward her. Just as the bolt was going to strike Nadia, Damien stepped in front of the bolt; his body absorbed the full blast. Just as he did that, the irises in his eyes disappeared and his eyes started to glow brightly.

Everyone could feel the energy surrounding Damien. They all stood in disbelief. The speed he moved to catch the electricity was amazing. He was faster than anything they had ever seen. But their amazement was short-lived by the imminent danger that they were about to face.

Just when they thought that it was all over, it seemed that it had only just begun. The electricity started to rage on ever more violently forcing Christian and Nadia to take cover as objects began to fly throughout the room. Damien stood still absorbing most of the lightning strikes and was seemingly unfazed while Cyris and Diamond stood firm in their places. Everything seemed like a bad electrical storm when, out of nowhere, a small wormhole appeared in the middle of the lab. No one could believe it. One thing they all knew for sure, though; whatever was on the other side wasn't friendly. It wasn't going to be fair and they knew that it would be out for blood.

A fight was definitely on its way...

CHAPTER 14

As the portal opened slowly, Christian and Nadia were immediately terrified. Damien, Diamond, and Cyris, all stood poised, ready for whatever would come through the wormhole. As he stood ready, Damien's body was surrounded by an immense, electrical aura. The electricity surrounding him had an intense effect on the equipment around them, sending them all into a frenzy of lights and sounds. His eyes glowed a bright, white color while his skin burned a deep red and an electrical current flowed around and through him. His body began to tremble violently at the power that coursed through him as he stood focused.

No one could understand what to make of this moment. The strange things that were happening to Damien over the last few days, the portal opening in the middle of the lab, and now the energy that emanated from his body – everything now seemed to add up. But everyone was troubled, too, at the sight of Damien and what he was becoming. What could it all mean?

Christian ran over to the device despite the immediate danger figuring that there was only one thing that he could do.

"What are you doing?" Damien yelled.

"We need to close it up," he answered. Christian tried everything that he could to shut the wormhole down. He pressed every button and flipped every switch that he saw, but it was all to no avail. "Ugh! Nothing is working!" he exclaimed in frustration.

Damien quickly grew impatient and grabbed Christian and threw him to the side.

"Damien, wait," Christian yelled.

The portal started to open wider by the second, and a very loud screech could be heard from the other side. The sound pierced their ears and sunk to their core. Right away, they knew what the sound was.

Damien looked over to Christian. "Take Nadia and get out of here." But all Christian could do was stand at the console frozen in fear. "DO IT! NOW!"

Christian rushed over and took Nadia by the hand. He did everything that he could to get her clear of the room and out of immediate danger, but Nadia fought it as much as she could until Damien walked over to her.

"I made a promise to myself that I would keep you safe, Nadia, no matter what. I intend to keep that promise." He caressed her face as she began to cry. "I love you, Nadia Montgomery. But you need to leave, now, and let me handle this. I'll find you later."

The sounds from the portal got louder with each passing second. Diamond looked over to Damien with grave concern. She knew that it was only a matter of time. "Damien..." she called out with uneasiness in her voice.

"Christian," Damien said, "get her out of here, now! I'll find you both later." With that, Christian and Nadia made a hasty retreat to find safety. They ran down the hallway leading away from the lab shouting out warnings. "Leave the area, now! Everyone, get to safety!" While running down the hall, Christian stopped in his tracks.

"What are you doing?" Nadia questioned.

On the wall was a handle surrounded by glass that read, "In Case of Emergency, Shatter Glass and Pull Handle." Thinking that it would be the fastest and most efficient way to force everyone to safety, Christian took the hammer on the side of the case, smashed the glass with it, and pulled the handle. Once the alarm sounded, they continued to run away.

Once they made their escape, the wormhole in the lab opened as tall as the room. The winds and the lightning grew more and more intense as time went on. So, Damien, Diamond, and Cyris, all braced themselves for a long fight as the screeches from the portal increased and got louder and more frequent. The piercing sound of the Night-stalkers shattered monitors and beakers leaving chemicals on the floor and the lab in disarray. Immediately though, Damien's body began to absorb the electricity in the air, and the aura surrounding him started pulsating with more intensity.

Then the worse finally happened... Floods of Night-stalkers filled the room, storming every corner, and wreaking havoc and chaos. Damien, right away, led the assault and a battle ensued in the middle of the lab. The fight was as intense and visceral as could be. Each of them fought three to four at a time without any let-up. The fight was nothing short of overwhelming for both Diamond and Cyris. They fought with everything they had and threw everything that they could at the creatures, but they were both tiring out quickly and growing weary.

Damien, however, was in another class. It was easy to tell that this wasn't the same man that fought the Night-stalkers at the mall. His ferocity matched the monsters tenfold, and he was able to stand on his own. Each blow that he delivered was accompanied by something more - either a burst of fire or lightning. He had never felt anything like it. The adrenaline flowed through him, and he intensified even more. His eyes continued to glow a bright white as the electricity surrounding him got more violent.

As they fought, Cyris noticed the changes in Damien, also. It reminded him of something quite familiar but also terrifying. It brought him back to the time that Damien and Diamond trained together. Only, he couldn't make out if this was the climax of it or just the beginning. But it also reminded him of the day that everything changed for the people of earth because it was at that moment, he saw firsthand the power that Dante held. And realizing what they were facing when it came to Damien, worried Cyris.

Meanwhile, Diamond, in a heated battle, pulled out her twin sai and used them to perfection. What made for a great defensive weapon doubled equally as an offensive one. For every blocked attack, an attack of her own directly followed, making it difficult for the Stalkers to get the upper hand.

She quickly got into a rhythm and strung her attacks together fluidly. She got comfortable in the fight. That's when, unexpectedly, Diamond was grabbed from behind by one of the creatures and the others began attacking her with malice and intent on killing her. As they beat her to near unconsciousness, Cyris looked over and saw that she was in trouble.

"Damien," Cyris screamed out, "we need to get to Diamond!"

Damien, growing more violent and furious, screamed aloud and intense energy came from his fingertips. Within an instant, he managed to electrocute the Night-stalkers that he was fighting until nothing remained but ashes. Afterward, he leaped into the air towards Cyris and called out to him for a boost. Cyris then propelled him off his hands and Damien flew towards the ones holding Diamond. As he did that, his entire body ignited in flames fully engulfing him.

He flew directly through one of them, killing it instantly. When he landed, he started taking all of them out one by one. An electrified fire came from every hit as his rage manifested in his attacks. Once he finally finished taking down the others surrounding Diamond, he turned his attention to the one holding her hostage. As he walked toward it, it started to back up slowly while still holding onto Diamond. As it backed away, it snarled and roared to intimidate Damien. But he continued to approach unfazed by its tactics. Abruptly, Damien disappeared.

Diamond couldn't believe what she was seeing. He was faster than anything she had ever seen before. Where could he have gone to? The creature, realizing that something wasn't right, looked to both sides as it continued to back away with Diamond still in its arms. That's when it felt something stop it at its back...

It was Damien standing back-to-back with it. With a slight whisper, he said, "I'm here," as he grabbed its tail and forced it to let Diamond go. Once it released her from its grasp, Damien leaped into the air with it and slammed it to the ground, and came down after it, forcing his fiery fist into the Night-stalker's stomach killing it instantly.

Immediately afterward, just when the fight seemed to be over, a large army of Night-stalkers came through the rift and filled the room. Their screeching echoed throughout the room and down the halls. Damien quickly grew tired of the fight. He needed a way to end it and end it quickly before matters got worse and the hoard escaped into the rest of the crowded complex. That's when it hit him...

"Cyris and Diamond, get down, now!" he shouted. "Get cover!"

Once they hid underneath a large table, Damien began to levitate slowly. As he rose into the air, his body began to rotate and the electric energy surrounding him grew more uncontrollable. Cyris and Diamond both tried to see what was happening to Damien but it was too much and far too dangerous. The lights in the room started to explode one after the other while different instruments flew across the room at high speeds. Suddenly, a burst of energy came from Damien unlike anything that they had ever seen, and he started to electrocute all the Night-stalkers until they, too, were reduced to nothing but ashes. Then, he fell to the floor to his knees and took the time to catch his breath.

Diamond and Cyris rushed to his side as soon as it was over, and they knew it was safe. As Damien looked up, they could see that the glow in his eyes had gone. Cyris, then reached out to comfort Damien.

"Don't touch me!" Damien exclaimed. "Please, don't touch me."

Cyris could feel the heat still coming from Damien as he drew his hand back. It was as if his skin was on fire. Diamond, meanwhile, ran over to turn the machine off and closed the portal finally. Then... a rattle. It was another Night-stalker and it had run out of the lab into the rest of the complex. Damien's eyes at once started to glow again and, before they knew it, he disappeared after it, leaving behind a trail of fire on the ground and static electricity in the air.

When Cyris and Diamond finally caught up with Damien, he was halfway down the hallway standing over the Night-stalker. It, just like the others, was dead. As he stood there, he breathed heavily trying to grasp what happened.

Cyris walked up to him.

"You alright, son?"

"I'm good now. You?"

"I'm fine. Nothing I can't walk away from."

"Good." Damien looked over to Diamond. "Are you alright?"

"I'm a little banged up but I'll make it. You saved my life, Damien. Thank you."

"Don't mention it." Damien stepped away from the creature over to Cyris and Diamond. "Cyris, we need to move this thing and get it somewhere secure. It needs to be examined - studied. I mean, the full workup. This hit too close to home."

"I'll have it taken care of," Cyris said. He at once got on the radio to call for aid.

Diamond stepped in. "I'm going to figure out this wormhole situation and see if we can get it under control."

Damien agreed. With that, he left to be alone. As he walked away, every thought possible ran through his mind. He had a tough time coming to grips with it all.

At first, Damien just wandered aimlessly throughout the complex. He purposely avoided Nadia's room and the clinic. How could he explain to her what happened? How could he explain what was happening to him when he didn't fully understand it himself?

Eventually, his walking landed him in the parking garage. When he got there, he stood contemplating his next move. "Do I stay, or do I go," he thought to himself over and over. Damien felt a strong need to stay; a need to be everyone's protector. But deep down, in his heart, he knew he needed answers and he knew that he couldn't get them if he stayed. Damien knew where he had to go. But going there meant that he would have to face the past and the loss that he experienced during the Event. He needed to go home again. So, he got on his motorcycle and drove away.

CHaPTer 15

Back at the lab, Diamond and Cyris spent the next hour cleaning up. The encounter with the hoard of Night-stalkers left the laboratory in complete disarray. Not to mention, the battle exhausted them to the point that they could barely stand. Most of all, however, the encounter also proved that the wormhole device worked. And for that reason, they had reason to celebrate. Deep down, however, they knew that more work had to be done to get the device field ready. And while this may have been a plus in their book, one thing remained, though, that gave them pause: What exactly happened with Damien?

It was all strange to them. The electrical energy, the fiery aura that surrounded Damien - everything that he could do was anything but normal. His speed, power, and tenacity were unlike anything they had ever seen.

Diamond walked over to the wormhole device. "So," she started, "am I the only one confused even a tiny bit by what just happened? I mean, nothing about what he did was, in any way, normal or within reason."

"There are clearly forces at work here that we don't fully under-stand," Cyris said. He walked over to Diamond and stood next to her. "Perhaps, there's more to Damien than we initially thought."

"You think?! Who can do things like that? Who moves that fast? And his eyes – who is he? What is he?"

"He's still one of us. He's one of the Pack. That hasn't changed. The way he fought to keep us safe – how he saved your life – it shows that he fights on the side of the people with us." Cyris rested his hand on her shoulder. "Look, I'm sure Damien is trying to figure out all of this as well. God, the boy is probably scared out of his mind right now."

Diamond took a deep breath and exhaled. "I know you're right. I guess it's just my nerves are bad right now. This was all too close. I'd hate to think of what could've happened if Damien hadn't been here."

"It could've been much worse," Cyris said. "Thankfully, we man-aged to get out of it with only some minor cuts and some damaged equipment. This could've ended a lot differently."

At that moment, Christian walked in. "Jeez, what in the world happened in here?"

Diamond looked at Christian and answered, "The portal, Night-stalkers, Damien. Take your pick."

Christian was confused. "Come again? What happened with Damien?"

"Well, you saw him," Diamond answered.

Cyris stepped in. "It's what you both didn't see that concerns me."

Christian sat down. "What do you mean?"

"The day of the Event, I saw some things. A lot of strange and... unexplainable things." Diamond stopped what she was doing and sat next to Christian. Cyris continued, "I was there when the first

Night-stalkers came through the portal. By now, that part isn't news. They ripped through everything breathing. It was sheer madness... and terror... My entire squad perished in a matter of minutes. I was only knocked out. I woke up not too long after that. Probably within minutes. And when I finally woke up, Dante was standing there. He stood right over me as he just decimated everything in his path. But this is the part I never told anyone. After he told me that the world would end, he made sure that it happened. God, I remember it all too well. Once he was done taunting me, Dante stretched out his hand. The next thing I know, the entire world was on fire. He had power unlike anything I had ever seen. Fire came straight from his hands, and he controlled it, manipulated it. It was the most terrifying thing I had ever seen. And I thought that I would never see that kind of power again – that is, until today. What I saw in Damien was so familiar, so vivid. The literal fire that came from him, the lightning-like speed that he showed, the electricity, all of it, I'm convinced, is tied to Dante in some way."

"Do you think they could be blood-related? Like brothers?" Diamond inquired.

"No, I don't think so," Cyris replied. "The gruff in Dante's voice leads me to think he's a bit older. Maybe about twenty years or so."

Diamond stood up angry and frustrated. "That puts us right back at square one! We still don't know anything!"

Christian got up to comfort her. "We will. We'll get the answers we need and the answers Damien needs. That's my brother out there. So, I'll walk to the end of the line and beyond with him if I need to. But if anyone can figure all this out, it's him."

While comforting Diamond, Christian heard the faint sound of a woman sobbing outside of the lab. Immediately, he went to see who it was. When he got into the hallway, he saw that it was Nadia sitting on the floor next to the door in tears. As he sat down beside her, he put his arm around her to give her comfort as well.

"Why is all of this happening?" she cried out. "I can't help him, Christian. I don't know how. I'm a doctor and I can't help him."

Christian asked her, "You love him, right?"

To which she replied, "Of course I do. I think I loved him since the first time I saw him."

Christian took off his glasses and rested his head on the wall. "Just be there for him. That's the best thing that you can do right now. He's gonna need all of us. I'm sure he doesn't quite understand everything that's happening to him either. But if anything, he should understand that all of us have his back. He's not alone and he knows that."

Nadia wiped her tears away. "I see why you're his best friend."

"Well, the guy kinda just grows on you, you know? Sort of like a bad rash," Christian said jokingly. "But he's a good guy. One thing I've learned over the past two years is that he's probably the most loyal and dependable person that you could ever meet. Very protective, too."

Nadia laughed. "Yeah, I noticed that. Thanks, Chris. How about we go figure out this portal situation?"

Throughout the next couple of hours, they all worked hard at getting the lab back in order and making the necessary repairs and alterations to the wormhole device to get it field-ready. Every second was spent working on algorithms and formulas. Everyone understood that there was no time to waste. So, fixing the device was the top priority.

No one in the room would say it but the silence in the room spoke volumes. They were all concerned about Damien and his well-being, both mentally and physically. They couldn't deny being amazed at what he could do. The power he possessed was awe-inspiring. But at the same time, deep down inside, they knew that, if they were not careful, any move could be Damien's last. Unfortunately, no one knew where to find him or how to help him if they didn't know where to find him.

Damien's silent exit spoke volumes to Cyris. He had begun to look at Damien as sort of an adoptive son in the same way that he looked at Diamond – though he would never utter those words out loud. But he felt that deeply for Damien. He had begun to love him as he would his own. How could he help him? What could he teach him to prepare him for the road ahead? These were only a few things that weighed on his mind and heart.

Diamond was more so left thankful. Damien saved her life. But at the same time, she was terrified by what she witnessed. She had never seen anything like it – not even on the day of the Event. His power and abilities took her by surprise. She took solace in Cyris' words, however. Knowing that he spoke from a place of experience and truth, eased her worries. She was comfortable enough now to know that Damien was on their side and that he would be there to protect them all.

For Christian, hearing about what Damien did caused him to ask questions within himself. Where did Damien's power come from? What triggered it? Could he do it again? But more than anything else, he was only concerned for his friend. Damien was someone that had saved his life many times and took care of him. They were like brothers. The two men shared an unbreakable bond and he would stand with him through whatever they faced. But now his brother faced a challenge ahead so difficult to even understand, that he could only face it alone, and that bothered Christian to no end.

Nadia did the best that she could do to remain strong. She knew that she was overwhelmed, though. An onslaught of emotions filled her up, and she could feel the tension of it in the pit of her stomach. Confusion, sadness, anger, hopelessness – to feel all of this at once was more than what she was used to even in these dark times. It was evident to everyone that she was worried about what would or could happen to Damien. Still, she remained focused on the task at hand - fixing the wormhole device.

Cyris turned to Christian. "How far have you gotten?"

"A few more tweaks, and I think the stabilization component will be ready. What about you guys?"

"I just got off the radio with the supply department," Cyris answered. "They're bringing a few new monitors down to replace these smashed-up ones."

"It's a good thing that I made that run the other day," Christian joked.

"I honestly don't know how you all can be so relaxed right now," Diamond stated. "I really don't. This was too close to home. I'm scared. I'm pissed. All I want to do right now is hit something." She threw her screwdriver to the floor. "Like, I'm literally two seconds away from having an entire meltdown. How are y'all so cool right now?"

Nadia walked over to her and sat her down. "Trust me. We're far from good or cool right now. But we have to keep our cool. It's the only way we get through this."

Cyris and Christian joined them in the conversation.

"She's right," Cyris said. "We all have something to lose. We lost a lot over the years. But at the end of it all, we have each other and, more importantly, we have an obligation to the world to see this through and end it."

Christian pulled up a chair, sat down, and had Diamond rest her head on his shoulders. "Think of it like this, after all of this is said and done, we can all breathe a little and just relax. Tell you what, how about we hit Lake Michigan and we all celebrate, just you, me, Nadia, and Cyris. We'll all have something to look forward to."

Reluctantly, Diamond smiled and agreed. "I'll hold you all to that. Thanks, guys."

Christian and Nadia continued working side by side crunching numbers on the calculations of the wormhole itself. The endgame was to send Dante and his horde of Night-stalkers back to where they came from. While they stayed busy doing that, Diamond and Cyris worked on the device itself. They understood that they needed to, not only be able to open it, but once it was open, they would need to be able to control it, sustain it, and shut it down all on command.

Everyone knew that they had a long way to go. So, they all worked diligently throughout the day. Their drive and ambition had never been clearer. They knew what needed to be done. Only one question remained, however. Where was Damien? No one knew. One thing was for certain, though. They wouldn't give up their quest to rid the world of Dante forever and they won't give up on Damien either. They knew he would be back, and they would be waiting for him.

CHAPTER 16

As Damien drove through the city, his mind raced as fast as his motorcycle. He needed answers. For him, his entire life had turned upside down for the second time in a matter of minutes. To go from a comfortable life with his mother and father and his baby sister to end up on his own in a world of darkness, and now these unknown changes within himself was a lot to take in. He was scared – scared about what was going on and, even more so, scared of what he was becoming.

Eventually, he found himself at his childhood home again. As he stopped and got off the motorcycle, he stood in what remained of the driveway and stared at the house. The nearly destroyed house stood as a reminder of not only the life that he had but of the changes that brought about his current situation. The two years that had passed up until this point had shaped him in ways that he never thought possible.

He walked up slowly to the front steps while removing his jacket and sat down. "What am I doing here?" he thought to himself. He couldn't fully understand what led him here. Was it familiarity? Comfort? He couldn't figure it out.

As he sat there on the front porch, he started having flashbacks to when he and his sister used to play in front of the house. He thought back to the times when he taught his sister how to ride a bike, how to climb a tree, how to fight - all the memories that he held close to him. They all came back to him in an instant.

"What am I doing here?" he thought to himself.

In the background, he could hear a faint voice call out to him. "Damien," it whispered.

"Am I losing it?" he pondered.

As the wind rustled through the bushes blowing the leaves on the ground about, he could hear the voice again, but more loudly. "Damien!" He finally stood up to have a look around outside of the house. He searched the side of the house between his and the next and no one was there. As he approached the backyard, he heard the call again increasing in intensity. That's when he finally heard, "DAMIEN!" At that moment, he realized that the voice wasn't coming from the outside... It was inside the house.

Damien walked up the deck leading to the kitchen, smashed the glass, and went inside the house to investigate. He immediately pulled out one of his daggers to prepare himself for whatever came next. He did his best to tread lightly through the heavily damaged kitchen and front entryway in hopes of the floor not caving into the basement. Nothing was found though. There was no trace of where the voice came from. He then inched up the creaky stairs in hope of not creating too much noise. Inch by inch he walked up to the top stair when, CRASH, right through the floor.

Damien hung on as hard as he could to a broken wood beam. He knew that if he dropped, then that would be his certain death. So, he tried hard to pull himself up, but it was to no avail. The wood beams were covered in water making it hard to get a firm grip. He looked down to see if it would've been at all safe so he could let go, but it was no use. Falling would've taken him on a direct path to the basement floor two levels below him.

"This can't end like this," he said out loud as he continued to struggle. But Damien was losing the fight - and he knew it. Soon after, Damien lost his grip. "This is it," he thought. Then, out of nowhere, a hand reached out, grabbed him, and pulled him up to safety.

Damien fell to his knees and started to clean himself off. "Really... you just don't know how much I appreciate you right now."

"Oh, I can imagine," the voice said.

Damien couldn't believe what he was hearing. It was a very familiar voice. As Damien looked up, he saw the long black coat flowing down to the floor. As he stood up, he looked the man straight in the eyes - at least what he could see of them. It was Dante!

Damien's rage built up in an instant at the sight of him. His eyes started to glow white, like what happened in the laboratory. In a fit of anger, Damien grabbed Dante by his throat, lifted him into the air, and threw him into the wall.

"What are you doing here?" Damien asked of him. He threw him to the ground and shouted, "Answer me!"

Dante got up and brushed off his coat. He then, removed his hood to reveal his full skull mask. On the side of his head, you could see nothing but severe burns from front to back. The look in his eyes was a cold glare. It was enough to make anyone uncomfortable.

"I didn't come for a fight, Damien. Only to talk," Dante said.

"Talk? What makes you think that I'll be interested in anything that you have to say?"

"Because I'm the only one on this god-forsaken planet who knows exactly what's happening to you."

Damien brushed his clothes off and decided to entertain Dante's thoughts as they walked back downstairs and outside to the front of the house. As the two men walked down the street through Damien's old neighborhood, silence filled the air. The streets were deserted compared to what they would usually be. The tension couldn't be more between them.

Damien quickly grew impatient. "You wanted to talk? So, talk. Why are you so quiet?"

"Ah, Damien," Dante began, "haven't you ever just taken the time to take in your surroundings? I mean, just absorb it?"

"Yeah, I have. Plenty of times... before you destroyed everyone's lives."

"Is that what you think I've done?"

Damien clenched his fists in frustration, trying not to let his anger show. "I had a good life before you came here," he began. "I lost everything because of you. My parents, my sister... it's all gone. Everyone living today lost everything because of you. Tell me, at what point am I wrong? You destroyed our world, left most of us to die, and unleashed your monsters on us every night... So yeah. That's exactly what I think!"

Dante eventually led Damien to a park near the house and they both sat down on the bleachers of a baseball diamond.

"Inside of you, Damien is a power unlike anything you've ever known. The lightning and fire are just a manifestation of that power."

"But where did it come from? Why me?" Damien inquired.

"It's in your DNA," Dante replied. "It's all genetic. But from what I can see, you haven't fully developed your powers yet. I honestly thought that you would have by now. What are you? Twenty? It started at eighteen for me. You see, where I'm from, the birth of the full manifestation of these abilities is called the Awakening. It's a painful process but one that comes with great rewards, also." Dante opened his hand and a small flame formed from it. "As I expected of you, I first gained my abilities at the age of eighteen. I was... scared, to say the least. I never knew such power. My parents found out eventually. My mother had walked in on me testing myself – testing my limits – and she got scared. That's when she ran to tell my father. They kicked me out shortly after. Claimed I was a freak of nature and I deserved to be cast out. So, I roamed the streets for days until someone found me. As it turns out, he had been searching for me for quite some time. He had heard about the young man living on the street who could do 'amazing things' with fire. He eventually gave me cooked food and a roof over my head. From then on, he had my loyalty." He got up.

Dante continued, "He trained me on how to fully harness my abilities and use them to bend the world to my will. Soon, he taught me quantum physics and I developed a way to open the gates of space and time - among other things, of course. That, my friend, was something that you and your little team clearly weren't ready for. My father eventually accepted me back in, but that was only after he developed abilities of his own. Then, he wanted to use me as a weapon. Come to find out, he was serving the same person that I was."

"So, you decided to use all of this to destroy our world?!" Damien asked angrily.

"No, Damien. I want to use them to rebuild. After seeing the fall of my world to the powers that be, I want to start anew and build a new world order. Yes, homes are destroyed. Yes, lives are lost, and families are ravaged. But the ends do truly justify my means. Centuries of rule and oppression and dictatorship and all of the promises that your corrupt politicians feed everyone every four years to get elected into an office to rule over a country that kills innocents for the color of their skin, unfounded prejudices, men who represent a white cloak and centuries-old ideologies just disguise themselves as businessmen and pillars of a community where your next door neighbor could just as easily be your unknown brother or want to kill you just for stepping on their lawn.

"All of the sugarcoating and hiding the real truths in order to satisfy their feeble, little desires and all those that follow behind... What is it all for? Security? A sense of peace? To make you feel good? NO! They're all illusions and constructs created to suppress the masses and fool them into thinking that their thoughts, opinions, and feelings actually mean something. No, Damien, to create something sustainable, you must upset the established order and tear down the preconceived notions that votes and elections, and democracy are a success and carry weight. It has failed time and time again in every world in every universe. And if need be, I will destroy everything and everyone in my path until the ultimate goal is complete. See, Damien, my purpose is so far ahead of you that you couldn't begin to comprehend it."

Damien, noticeably getting angrier by the second, stood up in a rage, fueled by Dante's words. "I comprehend enough. You're mad. You have really lost your mind. We didn't ask for ANY of this! We don't want your rulership. We don't want your new world order. You've done enough damage. And I'm going to stop you."

Dante found Damien's words amusing. "Join me, Damien. Don't be foolish. Why try to save these people? We're gods. Gods among men. They're all mere insects compared to what we could set out to accomplish."

Damien's rage began to overflow within him, and his eyes started to glow white. The irises of his eyes disappeared completely and the lightning aura around him started to form once more. Dante began to laugh in satisfaction. He wanted to push Damien to that point.

"Catch me," Dante whispered. And in an instant, he was gone. Damien quickly followed behind.

Their speeds were incredible. As Dante zipped from house to house, Damien stayed close on his trail. They were going so fast that they created fire trails on the ground, static charges, and rapid sonic booms.

Damien was able to keep up with Dante without any problem. The chase lasted for minutes until they finally ended up on the rooftop of an old nearby grocery store.

"This is your last chance, Damien," Dante said. "Join me or perish!"

Damien stood with the same lightning field around him. "I'd rather die."

"THEN SO BE IT!" With that, Dante reached his hand into the sky. The skies immediately turned black with dark clouds. As the rain began to fall, he created a bolt of lightning and hurled it at Damien.

Damien's sense of reality had started to slow down to a crawling speed. This enabled him to see the bolt coming at a tremendous speed, dodge it by leaping into the air and charging towards Dante with a flaming, lightning fist. But Dante was much faster. As he avoided the attack from Damien, Dante grabbed Damien's arm and threw him to the ground. He then grabbed him by the collar of his jacket, zoomed back in front of Damien's childhood home, and threw him to the ground.

"This is my world now, Damien. Look around you and see what I've wrought on the Earth. Your world and everything you know is finished!" And then he was gone.

Once Damien stood up, the rain stopped. He looked around in search of Dante, but he was nowhere in sight. He could only hear his faint, maniacal laugh far off in the distance. He ran to his motorcycle and drove off to go back to the headquarters.

When he made it back to the complex, Damien immediately went to his room and locked the door. He paced back and forth for minutes before he finally sat to relax. As he sat down, he became fatigued. So, he laid back on the bed and shut his eyes to get some rest. Rest was far from what he got, however.

When he closed his eyes, he started to hear a voice in his head call out to him. "Damien... Damien!" the voice called out. When he stood up and opened his eyes, he stood atop a dusty hill. Looking out into the distance, he saw the city ablaze in the night sky. "What am I seeing?" he thought. "Am I dreaming again?" Everything seemed so real to him, but he couldn't explain it.

Just when he closed his eyes again, he heard a knock at the door, and just like that, the vision was gone.

"Damien, it's me. Please, let me in." It was the voice of Nadia. He rushed to let her in and embraced her with tears in his eyes.

"What's wrong?" she asked.

"I need you to sit down." They both sat on the bed and Damien let out a deep sigh as he began to explain to her exactly what he had learned and all that he was experiencing. Surely, they were in for a long night as Damien started giving her every detail.

CHAPTER 17

The last couple of weeks had been stressful for everyone at the bunker. The team's nerves were bad, and the entire complex was on edge. Christian and Diamond worked nonstop on the wormhole device to perfect it and get it ready for the field. They would sometimes work for over twenty-four hours straight and sacrificed meals and leisure. Nadia split her time between the clinic and being with Damien. They felt the need to stay close and spend as much time together because they knew that they faced constant danger daily. In between those times, Damien and Cyris spent much of their time training and preparing themselves for what lay ahead. Everyone had their hands busy in one way or another.

While everyone was still replaying the events that unfolded in the laboratory in their minds, Damien was still trying to wrap his head around the confrontation that he had with Dante. As much as he wanted to embrace his powers, at the same time, they frightened him to no end. He couldn't use them comfortably without wondering to himself if he is, indeed, the real threat. And even more so, after hearing Dante's rant, he couldn't help but wonder what was Dante's ultimate goal. What was it that he was trying to achieve?

A month passed since the incidents in the lab and at Damien's home, and the team was completely drained. There was no word further from Dante, and the Night-stalkers had gone silent. And as much as they appreciated the quiet, they knew that there was more on the horizon and they would need to be ready for whatever came their way.

Working and training left little time for them to enjoy themselves and live life. After all, what reason was there to fight if they didn't have anything to fight for or something to remind them? So, Nadia, being the most light-hearted person in the Pack, decided to get everyone together — both the adults and children — to go out to one of the old beachfronts in the city and have a day of nothing but fun and games.

Nadia had been planning for everyone to go above ground and enjoy the lakefront. Even through all the destruction, the Chicago skyline remained a beautiful sight. After being wound up for weeks, everyone needed some serious rest and relaxation.

Knock knock!

"Hold on," Damien grunted as he rolled over from a good night's sleep.

As he got out of bed, he slipped on some clothes and went to the door. He opened it to find Nadia there with Christian right behind her.

She slipped in and gave Damien a quick kiss and sat on the bed. Christian went in right behind her.

"What are you still doing in bed?" she inquired. "Don't tell me you forgot..."

"Nah, nah," Damien answered as he wiped the crust from his eyes. "I just overslept."

Christian jumped in. "Come on, bro. Get ready. I haven't played basketball in a long time, and I promise you I'm about to school you today," he said laughing.

"Bro, you got yourself a game. Who's cooking? I hear Cyris is gonna throw something on the grill."

"That's what I heard, too," Nadia said. "I can't wait. I'm hungry."

"Give me a minute. Let me get ready."

As Damien went to the bathroom, Christian and Nadia left the room. He got in the shower and stood for a while and let the water run over him. This day had been planned for over a week now, but given the recent events, Damien wasn't sure if now was the time to have fun and let his guard down. However, since Nadia and Christian - the two most important people in his life - were looking forward to it, he decided to make the best of it.

A few minutes later, Damien met everyone in the cafeteria. Diamond had already begun to get everyone lined up into various groups to keep track of everyone, especially the children. They were all a lot more excited than the adults because they were finally going to get the opportunity to go outside and play for a while as kids should.

They didn't go far from the base. There was a park not too far away that was left somewhat intact after the Event. The children couldn't wait to run wild. All the adults stood by smiling because they could remember what it was like when they were kids; it was a time when they were able to enjoy the fresh air and play outside all day long.

Damien stood off in the distance and watched over everyone. As he thought back to his childhood, he remembered what it was like to have family, and he thought of the good times that he had with his parents and sister. He couldn't help but crack a smile. To see the children enjoy themselves and play freely, warmed his heart and helped him to remember what it was that they were all fighting for. For a time, everyone was able to breathe and take it all in because it was the break from the norm – the chaos – that everyone needed.

Christian walked up to Damien and stood next to him for a minute. "Feels good, doesn't it? To take a break from the madness?"

"Yeah. Yeah, it does." Damien let out a deep sigh. "I just need every day to be like this. Peaceful. Calm. Not looking over your shoulder all the time. You know, the simple things in life that we can sometimes take for granted." He gazed off at Nadia in the distance playing with the children. "To tell the truth, I can't wait until all of this is over so that I can settle down and start a family of my own, bro. This war with Dante; it's put a lot of things into perspective for me. Life is really too short. Before all of this, my family was important to me. But I was still a teenager. A stupid one at that. I didn't appreciate them like I should've. My parents, my sister; I should've shown them all more love. The last time I saw my baby sister, we got into a fight because she went into my room and took one of my CDs without asking me first. God, looking back at it now, it was all so trivial. It was only a CD. And I made a huge deal about it. Just as I going to apologize for how I acted with her, everything went down. The fire leading to her bedroom was too much. I couldn't get there to save her. I never got the chance to apologize to her."

"Look," Christian said, "I may not fully understand how you feel, but I can honestly say that you're doing a great job here protecting these people. I'm sure your sister and your parents would be proud."

"Damien!" Nadia called out to him as she walked up.

"I'll leave you two alone," Christian said as he left.

The couple kissed and then sat down on the grass. Nadia rested her head on his chest as he put his arm around her.

"How are you feeling?" Damien asked.

"I'm alright," she replied. "Just enjoying the fresh air. You know, I've been a little sick the past few days. I'm guessing it's just a stomach bug. But being out here is helping." Nadia turned to look at Damien. "I should be asking you how you're feeling. We haven't talked about what happened with you at the lab or about Dante. Are you sure you're alright?"

"Is this Dr. Montgomery talking or my girlfriend," Damien joked.

"I'm serious," she replied. "I need to know that you're alright. And I don't mean just physically."

"It's been a long month just processing everything," Damien started. "I'm not trying to leave you out of the loop or anything like that. I'm just processing. But I'm good... for now. I'm good here with you."

"But..."

Damien let out a sigh and said, "I'm not gonna lie to you. With all that's happened – Dante, the things that I was able to do against the Night-stalkers, it has me scared."

"Of what?"

"The future. Me. I'm scared of what I'm becoming. I want to protect you and everyone else. But am I the one everyone should be fearing? I mean... Dante, I know, is the immediate threat. But what about me? I don't want to be what he is. And I feel like that's what it's all leading to."

"And you won't, Damien," Nadia said sternly. "You're not him and he's not you. You're caring, compassionate, and most of all, you're my love. You're everything that Dante isn't."

Nadia's words made Damien feel better. That didn't mean that his fears weren't in the back of his mind. But rather than dwell on what-ifs, he decided that he would put that to the side and enjoy himself with all his friends – even if that joy was felt only for a day.

The two of them decided to get up and do some walking. A crisp breeze flowed throughout the park allowing them to relax and feel free. As they walked over to the basketball court, they could see Jimmy and some of the other kids playing a game with Cyris and Christian.

Damien quickly ran to join in the game while Nadia stood on the sidelines to watch along with Diamond. Both women couldn't help but smile. For the time being, everything seemed right yet surreal... it was a normal day. It was hard for anyone to imagine a life like this where they weren't hiding and living in fear. But here it was. They were living it at this moment, and everyone loved it.

Finally, the time came for everyone to go back inside. Once back at the base, everything was quiet again. Once all of the children laid down for bed, Cyris took the elevator to the roof. He stood there looking out over the city remembering what it once was, and he contemplated what it could be again.

All was quiet until he heard the elevator chime. It was Damien, Nadia, Christian, and Diamond. They all came and stood next to Cyris.

"I see you've found me," he said.

"Yeah," Diamond replied. "I figured this was where you were."

Cyris looked around at everyone. "What's up? Something wrong?"

"It's time we made a move," Damien said. "Get on the offense instead of always playing D."

The wind howled through the buildings.

"Today made it clear," Nadia said. "Things need to change for the better. We deserve more. These children and the rest of the world deserve more."

"But are you all ready to make the ultimate sacrifice if that moment comes?" Cyris asked. "Because I guarantee you that Dante will have no issue with sending us all to an early grave... quickly."

Christian interceded, "So, we come up with a plan and we stick to it. I can have the machine running in a few days. But whatever the plan is, we send that bastard, Dante, back to wherever it is he came from."

"Cyris, I'm gonna need your help controlling whatever this is inside of me. Help me to hone it in the right direction," Damien pleaded.

"Also, Cyris," Diamond started. "I think that it's time for you to take over leadership of the Pack. Honestly, I feel like I've gotten us as far as I can us."

"I saw this city fall with my very eyes," Cyris said. "I've dreamed for so long of a time when this war would be over. I've lost so much: my family, my friends, my troops. I'm not a leader. Not anymore. But Diamond, you've led the Pack successfully and I can't take that away from you. I won't. This group of people is yours. Christian, I haven't known you long, but I know that your genius will lead us into the future. Nadia, you've taken care of everyone here with tremendous care. We'll need that and more along the road ahead. And Damien, the fierce, selfless warrior; over the past few months, you've gone through many changes, but you managed to come out on top. Your strength and courage will be what takes us to victory. Tomorrow... we start preparations for the final assault."

With that, everyone agreed as they all looked out over the city realizing that soon, all of their worries and fears could be done away with, and rebuilding a promising future for everyone could be within reach.

CHAPTER 18

The following morning, everyone met in the conference room to discuss further plans. Even though the previous day was filled with joy and fun, they knew that those moments wouldn't mean much of anything unless they made it into more permanent conditions. The bottom line remained the same – the world needed to be rid of Dante's reign of terror forever.

As Damien, Christian, Diamond, and Nadia all sat down, Cyris stood at the head of the table to speak.

"My friends," he started, "we have come to a point in time where we need to fight back. Everything we have faced has led us all to this moment. All of us are together because of a common enemy. And that enemy is Dante. We have a name and face to our tormentor. And now, it's time for us to take him down. That being said, we need a permanent solution. One that'll rid this world of him forever. Now, we have one solution in progress and it's our most viable course of action. Christian, can you elaborate on that for us?"

"According to the data that was gathered by Damien and Nadia, Dante made it here through a wormhole that opened up in front of a building on the UIC campus. Now, Diamond and I have been working on a device that will replicate that same wormhole."

Diamond stepped in, "And as you all know, that device works, but only to a certain degree."

"What do you mean, 'to a certain degree'?" Nadia asked.

"We saw it working the day the Night-stalkers invaded and destroyed the lab," Christian. "But the stability of the wormhole isn't quite there yet. At this point, it could potentially do more harm than good."

"Do we have a time frame as to when it'll be ready to go?" Cyris inquired.

Christian looked down at his notes. "According to my calculations, two days. But that's if everything goes how I plan it to. I still need to figure out the stability issue. But I am hopeful."

Damien interrupted. "We still need to find him. I mean, honestly, there's no point in doing all of the planning if we still can't locate him. He could be anywhere in the city."

Cyris looked over to Damien and said, "I have an idea for that." Everyone sat up at full attention. "Now, we've all concluded that both you and Dante are linked somehow, Damien. There's no denying that. You both share the same, exact abilities. That brings me to my solution. There was a machine that was being developed here about ten years ago that would allow someone to link their mind with someone else's, even at great distances. Now, it's only a prototype. It never got tested in the field. I think now would be a perfect time to try it out. If something were to go wrong, I truly think that your body would be able to withstand it. But it's totally up to you. Also, Damien, I've thought of some specialized training just for you. I think we should get started right away."

Nadia immediately objected to that idea. "Cyris, that would mean unlocking whatever it is that Dante has? No! You can't! It's beyond not safe. As both his doctor and his girlfriend, I can't agree with it."

"From a military standpoint, we don't have a choice," Diamond suggested. "We need to, somehow, level the playing field. And this is possibly the best way of doing that. As much as it pains me to admit, we're severely outmatched in every way. Going in without some sort of trump card would be suicide."

Nadia gazes over at Damien - obviously concerned. "No, Damien. What if you can't control it? What if this power takes over? You can't put yourself at risk like that."

"There's no other way, babe. We can't beat him without some kind of edge. I am that edge. I've accepted that. We all have. I know what I need to do now. I need to be the one to take him down."

Tears began running down Nadia's face. "But what if you can't control it, Damien?"

"Then, you kill me. Take me off the board. The first sign of me going out of control, you kill me. No questions asked." Damien, then, looked over to Christian. "I want you to do it, Chris. You take my dagger." He pulled the dagger from his side and slid it across the table to Christian. "If anything goes wrong, bro, you put an end to it." He looked back over to Nadia and held her hand as he wiped the tears from her eyes. "You've gotta trust me on this, babe. It's the only way."

Silence filled the room as Nadia settled down. Everyone knew how high the stakes were. But without any other options, they all knew that they had no choice but to move forward with the plans as they were.

As everyone began to leave, Cyris stopped Damien before he could leave.

"Sit down, son. I need to talk to you."

They both sat down across from each other; each of them a little anxious.

"Damien," Cyris began, "you know the road that we're facing is a difficult one. Many of our people will die in battle. Unfortunately, there isn't a way around that. But out there in that field, I want those soldiers who are out there on the front line to look to you as their leader. I want them to follow you."

"But what about Diamond? She's the leader here. Not me."

"Yes, that's true. But she can't do the things that you can. She knows that."

"Does she know that we're having this conversation?"

"We talked about it at length before the meeting."

"You're serious? I'm not a leader. Not by a long shot." Damien pleaded with Cyris. "Don't do this, Cyris, please. I'm not that person."

Cyris stood up, walked around the table, and rested his hand on Damien's shoulder. "Son, that type of attitude is exactly why you should lead the soldiers into battle. You're a warrior, son - a good one at that. But you're humble and, most of all, you're caring. You will throw yourself in harm's way before you let your friends get hurt. I've seen that personally. That is the true definition of a leader. You've got this. I believe in you. Everyone here does. It's time for you to believe in yourself. Now, come on. We have a lot of work ahead of us.

With that, they both left the conference room and headed for the training room.

Meanwhile, in the laboratory, Diamond and Christian were hard at work on the wormhole device. Diamond stayed focused on the device itself and getting all of the mechanical issues fixed. Christian, however, was feeling the pressure of having to figure out the right equations to keep the portal open properly. His nervousness was beginning to show.

"What's wrong?" Diamond asked.

Christian sat his pencil down and wiped the sweat from his forehead. "I can't figure out the right equation that'll allow us to control the wormhole. Right now, at this point, I could get it to open. That's the easy part. The problem lies in being able to sustain the hole and shut it down on command."

Diamond sat beside him. "OK. So, what is it you think you're missing?"

"I don't know. I really don't. Alright, tell me if this makes sense. And maybe it's just me and I'm not seeing the picture clearly, but all logic is telling me that this formula should work for sustaining the portal without sacrificing control. At this point, the portal is going to suck everything in its path into it."

"Maybe it's just a matter of tweaking the equation a little bit," Diamond suggested. "What could sustain something this big and make it more stable?"

At last, it came to Christian. "Power! It needs more power! God, why didn't I see it before?"

"Are you sure?" Diamond asked.

Christian got up and began searching the laboratory. "It's the perfect solution. At first, I was only factoring in a minimal power source. That was just the power from the machine itself. But adding the extra voltage behind it would be enough to, not only open the portal but keep it open and stable for as long as we need it. It'll be like putting a harness and a muzzle around a wild dog. In this case, the extra electricity will act as that harness and muzzle on the wormhole, stabilizing it long enough to push Dante and his army back through."

Diamond at once started helping to look for a stronger power source. They searched through everything throughout the room.

After a few minutes of searching, Diamond finally came across something. "I found a car battery! It looks like it might've come off of a pickup truck. I'm not sure. Do you think this will be enough?"

"I don't know. Probably not," Christian said. "I need to see how much power it has. I think we may need a portable generator, too, to give it an extra boost."

"OK. I think that there's one of those in here somewhere."

After some careful searching, they finally found the generator. They both looked at each in excitement and eagerly anticipated what it could mean - not just for them personally, but for everyone on the planet.

As Christian had begun modifying the wormhole device with the new power sources, a calm came over him. The nervousness that he once felt when he and Damien first came to the Pack had left all of a sudden and had been replaced with a confidence he had never felt before in his life. Everything, for him at least, centered on this moment.

Once everything was connected, Christian picked up the device remote and he and Diamond stepped back behind a protective shield. They looked at each other and held hands as Christian started up the machine...

IT STARTED RIGHT AWAY!

Immediately, the portal opened up. Electricity flowed violently around the wormhole just as it did before. Only this time, after a minute, the wormhole stabilized. It worked! They couldn't believe it. It worked just as they had planned.

Christian couldn't wait to call everyone else to the lab. Still a bit concerned about everyone's safety, he decided that he should turn off the device until then. But his excitement boiled over as they waited for the rest of the team to get there.

He turned and looked at Diamond and said, "I couldn't have done it without you. Thank you. Look, I want you to know something now just in case I don't get to say it later."

Diamond was confused. "What is it?"

Just as he was about to start speaking, however, everyone started to arrive. It would have to wait...

"Tell me you have some good news, bro," Damien said.

"I know I said a couple of days earlier," Christian began. "However, it seems that I was overthinking the situation - a lot - when, in fact, the solution was so simple." He, then, used the remote to turn on the device. The wormhole opened up right in the middle of the lab. The stability couldn't have been any better.

Everyone stood in amazement. They were all so excited that they just stood there and hugged each other for a couple of minutes. They were all happy and full of hope.

Christian looked up and said, "This isn't even the best part of the day." As they broke away from the group hug, Christian took hold of Diamond's hand, looked her in the eyes, and said, "As I was trying to tell you, I couldn't have done this without you. We make a good team. Diamond, I don't want this to be the end of that. I don't want to go back to just being the smart guy or the nerd. I want a family." He, then, got down on one knee. "I want you to be the start of my new family. Marry me, Diamond. Help me to be great. Be my rock and my strength and, in turn, I'll be yours. Will you be my wife?"

Diamond was undoubtedly stunned along with everyone else. Her eyes glazed over as she began to tear up. And then, "YES! Yes, I'll marry you, Christian."

Everyone embraced once more as they celebrated the occasion.

"Everyone," Damien started, "I might as well keep the trend going." He turned to Nadia and, also, got down on one knee. "Nadia, you cared for me when I was at my lowest. You have been my support and backbone since we met. I've fallen for you, and I don't ever want to get up. It would be my greatest honor if you would be my wife."

Nadia immediately shed tears. She was overwhelmed with emotion. Finally, she managed to say, "Of course, I will, Damien."

BEEP! BEEP! BEEP!

Cyris looked down at his pocket monitor. "It seems we have more good news," he said. "We now have Dante's location. Damien, Diamond, we need to suit up now while we have the element of surprise. Christian, can you get the device mobile right away?"

"Yeah, that won't be a problem."

"Fine. Let's move out," Cyris ordered.

Damien kissed Nadia and looked into her eyes. "I love you. Let's build our future starting right now."

"I love you, too."

With that, Damien, Cyris, and Diamond hurried off to prepare for the attack. The future now rested in their hands.

CHAPTER 19

As everyone prepared for the assault, Damien spent his time in deep meditation. He spent hours in his room focusing on the task at hand and what their success could mean. He knew in his heart that there was only one way to bring peace back to the city of Chicago and the rest of the planet. For that to happen, Dante had to die, and he both wanted and needed to be the one to bring him to death.

As he suited up, he thought about everything and everyone that was lost over the years in the struggle: his parents, his sister, and everyone else on the planet that lost someone due to Dante's arrival. It invigorated him. It strengthened him and gave him a new sense of purpose. The life that he created while living with The Pack also gave him a new reason to live. He found a new family and managed to fall in love in the process. All these things combined gave him all the reason he needed to fight and put his body and life on the line.

After meditating, Damien made his way to the auditorium where the entire Pack community had met. All the civilians in attendance sat murmuring among themselves trying to figure out what was going on. Why was everyone gathered together? No one knew the answer. Damien eventually made his way backstage and ran into Diamond.

"Are you ready?" she asked.

"As ready as I'll ever be." The nervousness showed clearly on his face. It was a feeling that scared him far more than the fight that he knew was ahead.

"You'll go out with Cyris and when he's finished, you'll speak." Diamond rubbed him on his back comforting him and taking notice of his sheer nervousness. "Relax. You'll do fine. Get ready. We're about to start."

Diamond, then, stepped out onto the stage and started speaking.

"My fellow Pack members. We called this emergency meeting with all of you to keep you abreast of the situation at hand. There has been a lot going on behind the scenes that I'm sure you all have questions about. We're going to fill you all in now. To do that, I'll invite both Cyris and Damien to the stage."

Applause filled the air as Cyris and Damien stepped onto the stage. Damien stepped into the background as Cyris stood out in front of the podium.

As Cyris signaled for the crowd to be silent, he started to speak. "My brothers and sisters, I'm sure you're all wondering why we're gathered here today. I'll make it simple. We finally have a location of the person responsible for ruining our world - Dante. As he rests comfortably in a nearby downtown office atop the Willis Tower, our troops are ready to mobilize. It's time we take the fight to his doorstep. This is it, everyone. This is the moment that we've all been waiting for. We're facing the end of the war. Let's see it through."

Everyone gave thunderous applause as Cyris moved to the background and Damien stepped up. He stood there for a second as the applause got louder and more resonant. He spoke:

"Over the past two years, we've all suffered. We've lost loved ones. We have been forced to live underground and scratch and fend for whatever we can get. We've learned to not only survive but thrive. That's good. It means we're resilient. We're fighters, all of us. Quite frankly though, I'm tired. This isn't a way for anyone to live. You can't raise children in these times because they're so dangerous and full of peril. You know, when I was a kid, my safe place was my home. If I had a bad day at school, I knew that at the end of the day, I was going home. Now, our homes are lost to us. Everything that the world was before the Event is now gone. Gone but not forgotten. But I don't want it to just be a memory of times past. It needs to be the present again. That's what we're fighting for. We're fighting to build a future for the generations to come. So, we're going to kick down Dante's door and we're going to finally put his reign of terror to an end. There will be no more hiding. There will be no more running. True, some of us won't be coming back. But those sacrifices will not be made in vain. Remember... we're fighting for ourselves. We're fighting for our children. We're fighting for our right to live. We will succeed and we will carry on. But most of all... We'll be FREE!"

The crowd celebrated with a roar of support and stood up and applauded so loudly that it rocked the complex. Everyone was in so much excitement that it couldn't be held. Damien's speech did what it was supposed to do. And that was to motivate everyone to action.

The game was on now. As everyone converged to the hangar, excitement was felt everywhere. The soldiers inside the hangar hyped each other up as they prepared for the upcoming battle.

Once Diamond, Cyris, and Damien entered the room, everyone fell silent.

"Remember," Diamond began, "we're fighting for our freedom, soldiers. Fight hard. Fight bravely. But never give up. You got it?!"

All of the troops shouted in agreement.

Cyris commanded, "Let's move out!"

Cyris pulled Diamond, Christian, and Damien to the side. "Look, we need to stay in communication with each other for this to work." He handed everyone a small comms unit to put in their ear.

Nadia ran out to the hangar just as they were about to walk off. She, too, was dressed for battle. "Let's go."

"Wait a second," Damien said. "Where are you going?"

"If you're going out there, then so am I."

"No," Damien said adamantly.

"Look, I know you're just trying to protect me, but this is my fight, too. I'm going."

Against his better judgment, Damien relented, and Cyris handed her a comms unit.

Diamond and Christian loaded their truck with the wormhole device while Cyris and Nadia pulled out in an armored Pontiac TransAm. Damien got on his motorcycle and drove off as fast as he could.

As they made it to the surface, the daylight started to disappear gradually. Damien looked up in the sky and noticed the strangest thing - a wormhole in the middle of the sky directly above Willis Tower.

"You guys see that?" he asked.

Diamond replied, "How could you miss it?"

"Let's make our way to the Tower," Cyris said. "Diamond, prime the device."

With that, everyone made their way toward Willis Tower for a full assault. Along the way, the Night-stalkers were lined up along both sides of the road, but they were different. They weren't as primal or savage. They were much more reserved, more sentient almost.

As they arrived at the building, they could see exactly where the portal was coming from. It was directly above the Tower atop the two spires. The team and soldiers all stood around the street and stared at the wormhole. Damien got off his motorcycle as he pulled up and stood in amazement with everyone else at the anomaly above the city.

Immediately, Damien stepped out in front and took command. "Alright, it's time to split into teams. Alpha Team, led by Diamond, will take the front door and clear the lobby. Bravo Team, led by myself, will follow right behind them and take the fight directly to Dante at which point Alpha Team will become Bravo Team's backup. Charlie Team, led by Cyris, will cover the rear and go up the back. Delta Team, led by Christian, will stay on the ground. You'll get that device powered and ready to go as well as protecting the front door. Once we go in, nothing goes in or out. The objective is to get Dante through our wormhole and shut down his. Any questions?" Silence filled the air. "Alright, let's move it!"

As the teams took to their positions, the skies got darker, and the earth shook violently. The soldiers paused for a moment to regain their footing and then CHARGE! The war was on.

The first team stormed the entrance and opened fire on the Night-stalkers guarding the lobby. The first wave of creatures fell easily. A second wave came flooding down the stairs in full force. Diamond at once emptied clip after clip of her assault rifle until there was nothing left. The rest of her squad did the same. Soon enough, everyone was out of bullets and using knives and swords.

They all fought as hard as they could, but the sheer number of creatures proved to be too much. "Damien," Diamond shouted over the comms, "send your men in. Hurry!" With that, Damien and his unit stormed the lobby and began to take charge. Damien, fueled by anger, started to generate an electrical aura around him again as he fought. The power inside him and the uncontrollable rage he felt began to take over him as each blow that he delivered obliterated each one.

The soldiers couldn't believe what they were seeing. Damien was single-handedly taking on the Night-stalkers with ease. Fire and electricity blended blow for blow as he took down each one. Diamond, even though she had seen this power before, stood in awe of his abilities. Damien quickly dispatched them all and powered down. The soldiers cheered and shouted joyfully at the victory. But Damien stood there to regain his composure.

"Don't celebrate yet," he ordered. "We have a long way to go," Damien called Cyris over the radio. "Cyris, hold your men off at the door. If you go in hot, you'll get bombarded."

"What do you suggest?" Cyris inquired.

"We need a diversion to draw them out," Diamond suggested. "Damien, I know this is asking a lot, but can you create the fire on command?"

"I don't know. Maybe if I try hard enough I could. What do you have in mind?"

"Perhaps, if Christian could hack into the computer systems that are still active in the building, he could turn on the sprinkler system. Then, you create the fire to activate the alarm and sprinklers and flush them out on that end and Cyris and the Charlie Team can take out those Night-stalkers as they come out."

"My friends," Christian said over comms, "that idea is crazy enough that it just might work." Immediately, Christian started working on the computer systems.

"Look," Damien said, "I'm not gonna wait. I'll start to move quietly through the building with my team. Diamond, you come with me and keep your team here to guard the door."

With that, they started to make their way upstairs through the building. As Damien and his squad made their ascension, the lights flickered wildly all around them. The thunder crashing outside could be heard clearly as if it was happening right next to them. But they pressed forward towards their goal.

"Chris, what's the status of those computers?" Damien inquired.

"Almost there, bro. Just a few more minutes."

SWOOSH!

One of the soldiers turned around. "Hey, where did Hawkins go?"

The other soldiers stopped to look back and noticed that Hawkins was missing, too.

"Alright, everyone," Damien said, "Looks like we have company. Get ready."

"Damien, are you alright?" Nadia asked.

"Yeah, you and Cyris get ready. Chris, is everything a go?"

"We're set," Christian replied.

SWOOSH! SWOOSH!

Another two soldiers were taken. Damien could feel his blood boil with anger. In an instant, fire came from his hands, and he set one of the walls on fire forcing the sprinklers to come on. When the creatures came out, Damien pulled out his katana and sliced through both of them with ease leaving them cut in two and laying on the ground.

The plan was now set into motion. There was only one problem now... the building was now catching fire swiftly. The blaze spread faster than anyone could've possibly predicted. Fearing for the safety of the soldiers, Damien ordered everyone to make their way back downstairs and out of the building. Once they started to evacuate, Damien worked his way further up to the rooftop so that he could shut down Dante's portal.

Damien ran as hard as he could to the top. He tried communicating with everyone but got nothing but silence. His rage grew more and more as he reached the final few floors. He feared the worse because he had already lost people close to him and he didn't want to feel that pain again. So, he raced up the stairs past the 108th floor until he reached the rooftop.

He searched all around for the device that had the portal open above the city. It seemed impossible to find. Suddenly, he heard a sound - the sound of a muffled groan. As he turned around, he couldn't believe his eyes. It was his friends, his comrades - Nadia, Christian, Cyris, and Diamond - tied up to the portal machine.

"Damien, behind you," Nadia shouted.

Just as he could turn around... "Hello, Damien." Dante knocked him down to the ground. Dante walked over to the group and cut the ropes, releasing everyone... but he held onto Cyris.

"Look at all of you," Dante taunted. "You're pitiful. Desperately fighting to save a world that was already on the brink of destruction itself just before my arrival. You want peace? You want justice? Your world governments were on the brink of collapse prior to this. And you know the funny thing? It was the same on my world, and the next world, and the next world, and the next... but I figured it out. And even my master wasn't smart enough to figure it out. But I did." He looked up at the wormhole in the sky and, then, he looked back at them. "A reality merge. Merge the infinite realities into one. You see, throughout my travels among the different dimensions and timelines, I've taken notice of the one dominant quality of every person I've come across. Love was the strongest. A simple four-letter word held a connection so strong that one would sacrifice everything for this one emotion - much like how you all fight and sacrifice for each other. Truthfully, I admire that in all of you."

Dante continued, "However, it's time for your world and all others to end and a new one to begin." Dante looked down at Cyris as he continued to hold him captive. His body began to electrify as he removed his hood. His hand started to glow a bright red and formed a sharp energy blade. "I told you there was no surviving this."

"Dante," Damien cried, "Please, don't do this!"

Damien got up and ran to stop Dante, but he was far too late. Dante lifted Cyris high in the air and, with one huge thrust, he plunged his energy blade through Cyris' back. The blade pierced through his chest as Dante held him in the air before releasing him. As he fell to the ground, Damien made it over in time to catch him before he hit the ground. But it didn't matter. Cyris was already dead. Damien sat on the ground with Cyris' lifeless body in his arms.

Rest in peace to their fallen soldier: Major James Collins a.k.a. Cyris.

CHAPTER 20

The team all stood around in complete disbelief. Cyris, a man who had helped to lead the Pack for over two years, was now dead. Damien sat holding his lifeless body, filled with grief and remorse. Diamond bitterly wept in Christian's arms over the loss of the man who became her surrogate father. Nadia, who had become close to Cyris over the years, collapsed from the shock.

"What did you do?!" shouted Diamond.

"You all left me no choice," Dante said with a callous tone.

"There's always a choice," she replied. "You had a choice from the beginning. Every single thing that you've done to terrorize this planet was your choice."

Dante looked to the sky and paused for a moment. "I... I never had a choice. Ever since I developed these abilities, I was used as a weapon to serve others' purposes. Just a mere pawn in the scheme of power-hungry people who'll stop at nothing to see the world enslaved. No... no, my friend. It's liberation that I want — a liberation of the multiverse and a free society for all."

"But at what cost?" Nadia questioned. "When is this enough? Haven't you taken enough lives? Because of you, we live in fear every day. That isn't liberation. It's a slavery of both the body and the mind."

"Only if you lack the vision and commitment to see it through," Dante started. "To create a new society, you need to tear down the old institutions and start from scratch. Only then can a new world rise atop the ruins of the old society. Yes, I was a slave to that kind of thinking, too. It was never my goal to come here and destroy your world. What would be the purpose? What could I gain? But as I came through to your world, I was filled with a new calling. And that was to be free from the control of those who possess true power and influence. I must destroy the worlds that he created and start anew."

"You're insane!" Nadia shouted.

"No," Dante replied. "I am simply a man who has seen both the best and the worst of man. I will see success... And you all could've joined me. Now, you have to die!"

With that, Dante took to attacking the two women. Right away, Diamond and Nadia were on defense. Dante attacked viciously without mercy. Each blow meant to kill. However, the girls fought back just as hard matching Dante blow for blow.

Damien still held onto Cyris but, at the same time, he had begun to slip into a trance. The pupils in his eyes had disappeared as his eyes turned pure white and then started to glow a bright blue. His skin began to sizzle, and electricity surrounded him and engulfed his body as the roof started to crumble around him from the energy.

Lightning streamed across the dark sky as the thunder crashed. Nadia at once noticed what was going on with Damien. She tried running to his side but was quickly met with an army of Night-stalkers. As she did what she could to fight them off, the lightning began to strike Damien over and over again and with each bolt, his eyes would glow more. Nadia fought as hard as she could to get to Damien but the sheer number of them proved to be far too many.

Christian rushed for Dante's portal machine to try to shut it down. As much as he wanted to help his friend, he knew, deep down, that this was what Damien would've wanted him to do first. At first glance, Christian felt overwhelmed at the thought of crippling a device of this magnitude. He knew, however, he had no choice but to try because the stakes were far too great.

Diamond continued to fight Dante on her own. Vengeance clouded her mind, and she could think of nothing more. The only thing that she could see was Dante's death. It drove her to continue fighting even if it seemed as though the fight was an uphill one.

"I'll kill you!" she shouted out as she continued to strike at him.

Dante laughed at her, mocking her. To upset her further, he folded his arms and only used his legs to fight, toying with her. With every swing she threw, he'd tease and taunt her, forcing her to exert herself more and tire out.

"You don't have the heart to kill," Dante replied. "Not even me. I've looked deeply into your eyes, child, and I've read your soul. Inside, you're just a scared, helpless little girl and the leader of a lost cause."

Dante's reply only added fuel to Diamond's fire. So, she pulled out her sai and went on a full offensive. She sent out one vicious blow after another in hopes of delivering a fatal stab. In the same instance, Nadia still struggled with the Night-stalkers while Christian continued to try to shut down Dante's portal. It seemed that they faced a battle that was so far uphill it was too steep to climb. Everything they did, all their planning and efforts, seemed to fall apart.

Even though Diamond fought as hard as she could, Dante proved to be too much for her, and he quickly overpowered her as he was growing weary of toying with her. Diamond in a final effort to fight back struck at Dante with her sai but, using his super speed, he dodged the attack, grabbed both of her sai, and threw them to the ground.

"You fight well," he taunted just before knocking down Diamond. He rushed to Nadia, grabbed her by the neck, and hoisted her high in the air. "But not well enough. It's time to say goodbye, little ones."

The world began to shake intensely as the storm surrounding Damien grew more destructive. Lightning from above struck one of the spires on the rooftop and it collapsed onto the adjacent building and the ground below. Damien let out an agonizing scream as bolts of lightning struck him one after the other breaking him down to his hands and knees. Flames erupted from his back as Christian, Nadia, and Diamond looked on in horror at what was happening.

As the thunder crashed one more time, a huge bolt of lightning struck Damien again and he shouted out, "NO!", as he used his super speed to rush over to Dante and Diamond.

He grabbed Dante's arm and looked him in the eyes as his eyes glowed brightly.

"No one else dies, Dante," he commanded. "This ends here... between us."

He released his arm and stepped back as Dante dropped Diamond. She got up ready to fight again but Damien quickly stepped in front of her.

"No, Diamond," he said as he stared Dante down through his mask. "This fight is mine."

Dante laughed. "And so it is, Damien." Still staring Damien in the eyes, "Run along, little girl."

"Damien, you can't be serious. Let us help you," Diamond pleaded.

"It's alright. Right now, you need to help Nadia and Christian. Shut that generator down and get out of here. They still need you on the ground." Still, she hesitated. "Diamond, go... now."

Although frustrated, Diamond agreed and left Damien and Dante to themselves. The thunder continued to echo throughout the sky as the rain fell harder with each passing second. The tension was high between the two of them.

"Are you going to kill me, Damien?" Dante taunted.

"No," he replied. "I'm going to make to make you feel the pain of every innocent life you took and just when you think that I'm done and you've had enough, you'll beg me to kill you."

The two charged each other at a tremendous speed. When they met, their fists collided with the other's, and it caused a shockwave so powerful that it sent them and everything around them flying. Diamond and Nadia were among the ones knocked down along with the Night-stalkers. They both looked up in disbelief at what was just the first punch.

Dante rushed Damien again as he tried to regain his footing. When he reached him, Damien disappeared from in front of him through the clouds of smoke and showed up behind Dante, and struck him in the back, knocking him down. From there, Damien went for an all-out attack while Dante was on his knees. But Dante was a highly skilled fighter being able to counter every punch and kick with perfect accuracy eventually overtaking Damien and regaining the upper hand.

Meanwhile, the thunderstorm raged on with more intensity. Christian stopped working on the machine briefly and looked up at Damien and Dante and managed to notice something that he couldn't explain - they were the ones causing the storm to get worse. As they fought, Christian looked to the sky and became more aware of the growing threat. Through the wormhole, he could see ripples and images within those ripples. It was then that he realized the seriousness of the situation... He was looking at ripples of the different times and dimensions through the space-time continuum. Dante's plan was beginning to take shape.

"Diamond!" he called out. "Diamond!"

"I'm a little tied up at the moment," she answered as she continued to slay Night-stalkers.

"That's cool and all," he started, "but we have an even bigger problem."

Nadia looked up at the sky and stood in disbelief. "Is that what I think it is?"

As Diamond killed the last creature, she finally looked up at the sky. Once she realized how grave the situation was, she rushed over to help Christian as Nadia stood guard.

"Alright," Diamond started. "Did you try recalibrating the hardware or reformatting the software?"

"Didn't work."

"What about creating a virus code?"

"I tried that. But the software just rewrote itself to destroy the virus and make itself more powerful. It's almost like giving protein and weights to a bodybuilder. It just made it stronger. It fed off of it."

Diamond paused for a moment. "You know what? I've had enough of this." She pulled her sai out and stabbed the machine over and over again effectively shutting down the machine and closing the space-time ripple.

"Alright," Diamond said. "We need to get to the ground."

Nadia adamantly objected. "No! I'm not leaving without Damien."

"Diamond's right, Nadia," Christian agreed. "This isn't the place for us right now. I'm sure Dante noticed that the machine is shut down by now. We have to go. Besides, we'd just be a distraction to Damien."

Diamond rested her hand on Nadia's shoulder to give her comfort. She looked over at the intense battle between Damien and Dante and looked back at Nadia. "It's what he wanted. We have to go... now."

Against her judgment, Nadia agreed, and they all headed for the door.

Damien continued to fight as hard as he could against Dante. But Dante proved to be a lot tougher than he expected initially. The truth was, though, Damien was holding back to contain the collateral damage from the fight. Even though he wanted Dante to pay, the lives of his friends mattered to him more.

As Damien started gaining the upper hand, he noticed the others headed for the door to go back downstairs to the ground level. The problem was Dante had noticed them, too. In a fit of rage, Dante used an energy blast to knock Damien back, and almost at once, he sent out another one toward the door.

Damien tried to rush to deflect the blast before it reached the door, but he was too late. Just as Christian made it through the door, the energy slammed into the door and sealed it permanently.

"No!" Damien yelled out as he realized what had just happened.

"This building is coming down, Damien," Dante said. "And not only do I have you, but I have your precious love and your adorable leader as well. And while you and I may survive due to your finally experiencing the Awakening, I can't say the same for those two."

Nadia and Diamond both looked worried on the outside. The fear that they felt on the inside was far worse because they knew that at any moment it could be the end of their lives. And what was worse was that they felt that they couldn't help Damien at all. He was truly on his own as the war against Dante and his evil horde continued.

CHAPTER 21

Diamond and Nadia ran for cover as the rooftop started to collapse. The situation was becoming grimmer by the second as the fight between Damien and Dante became more intense. Every blow came with a force of electric energy that sacrificed the structural integrity of the building that they were on.

The women knew that at any moment they could die if they stayed during the battle. So, they began to look for a way down. They ran around the fight over to one side of the building where a scaffold had always been. When they got there, though, it was hanging on barely by a cable. Seeing that the scaffold wouldn't work, they ran over to another side of the building to see if there was another exit. But every direction proved to be blocked by a wall of fire. Everything was beginning to look hopeless and, with the door that they came in having collapsed, it appeared that there was no way down.

Everyone on the ground looked toward the top of the Tower as the fight went on. They couldn't see the battle itself. Only the flames and lightning. The amount of lightning in the sky striking the spires and the rooftop was a clear indication, however, that the fight was raging on. And there would be nothing that they could do about it from the ground.

Amid the fight, Damien noticed that Nadia and Diamond were trapped. He quickly knocked Dante to the ground and attempted to run to help them. However, Dante grabbed Damien by his ankle and pulled him down to the ground with him. He, then, rushed Damien, got on top of him, and hit him repeatedly in the face trying to knock him out.

Every hit caused the rooftop to break apart more. Damien's anger blazed against Dante as he started to lose control. Damien screamed at the top of his lungs as he then reversed Dante's attacks and began to pummel Dante into the concrete. But Dante just laughed in an almost hysterical and maniacal manner. He enjoyed it.

"You won't hurt anyone ever again," Damien declared.

Damien lifted Dante off the ground and slammed him into the shut door. In a quick burst of speed, Damien rushed towards Dante, grabbed him by the neck, hoisted him high in the air, and began a series of devastating blows to Dante's face. Damien's anger was more apparent by the second as he continued to un-leash blow after blow. He thought of his parents, his sister, Cyris, and the countless number of victims that Dante left in his wake. Eventually, all Damien could feel was hatred and vengeance. He wanted Dante dead.

Growing tired of Damien's onslaught, Dante began to charge up and generated an energy field to propel Damien away from him. Once he fell to the ground, he stood up, adjusted his mask, and took off his coat. Damien looked up at him with a defeated look on his face as Dante began to levitate himself. He hovered over him as he looked down at him. And as the women looked on, they both realized that Damien was in trouble.

"You see, Damien," he said. "You can't win. Not like this. You may have finally awakened, but you've barely tapped into what you can do. You're holding back. Don't, please. I want you to unleash it all. Let go of fear. Let go of restraint, of doubt. Dig deep, Damien..." He looked toward Nadia and Diamond. "...And protect those you love!"

Dante sent an electrical blast hurtling toward Nadia and Diamond. They stood in fear as it came flying toward them, thinking that this could be their final moment. Damien immediately gathered all his strength and rushed to their side and pushed them both out of the way as the blast hit, striking him in the chest instead.

"I told you, you're done hurting people," Damien said as he fell to the ground half-conscious.

Nadia ran over to care for Damien. She prayed over and over, hoping that he wasn't dead. As she embraced him, Damien appeared to be barely breathing, apparently winded and incapacitated from the blast.

As she began to cry, she caressed his face and said to him, "Damien, you can't leave me now. Do hear me? I need you here. We all need you here. We need you to fight. Use this gift you have and fight." Damien just lay in her arms - lifeless.

Dante glided over toward the three of them and started to charge up another blast. Nadia couldn't help but sit in terror at the thought of what Dante would do. They were all helpless against Dante who, at this point, appeared to be unstoppable. Just as Dante unleashed another attack at them, Diamond jumped between Dante and her friends and used her sai to block the lightning from striking them.

"Damien, wake up, please!" Nadia screamed out to him. "We need you!"

The thunderstorm got worse when a huge bolt of lightning came from the clouds toward Damien. When Nadia saw it coming, she jumped out of the way just as it struck him. His body began to generate a tremendous amount of energy. The energy surrounding him started to pulse as he began to sit up and Nadia and Diamond ran for cover.

He managed to get himself up on one knee and he looked up at Dante. "I've had enough of this," he said as he propelled himself into the air toward Dante and tackled him out of the sky. "You're finished!" he shouted. As he sped away, Damien immediately picked up where he left off pummeling Dante using all his strength and anger.

"I'll never let you hurt anyone else ever again," Damien said as he looked into his eyes. He picked him off the ground and held him in the air with one arm and continued hitting him with the other. Each hit got stronger as they became infused with the lightning and fire that he was generating.

Damien was getting the upper hand but, at the same time, he was losing control of himself. His anger and rage got the better of him. He was determined to beat Dante to within an inch of his life. As Nadia looked on, she noticed the fury that Damien displayed and ran to him.

"Nadia, no!" Diamond yelled out. "Stay back. It's too dangerous!"

But she didn't listen. She ran to him anyway.

Just as Damien was about to kill Dante, Nadia reached him and grabbed his arm.

"Damien, stop, please!" she pleaded. She stroked his back to calm him down. And as he looked up at her, she said, "This isn't you. You're not a killer. You're not him. Please, let's just get out of here."

Damien agreed, powered down, and got off of Dante. He looked at him and said, "She's right, you know? I'm not you. I understand your logic, Dante. I really do. I can even sympathize with you and what happened on your Earth. And I'm sorry that all of that happened to you and your world, Dante. But this is our home. We were fine here before you came, and we'll be fine here long after you're gone. You see, we're survivors, Dante, so we'll make it. It's time for you to go home."

Damien and Nadia turned around and walked away. As they made their way over to meet up with Diamond, they all felt a sense of relief. It was finally over with Dante. The war had been won.

"We need to find a way down," Damien said. "This building is going to come down within minutes."

"There's a fire escape blocked off by some rubble near where I was hiding," Diamond suggested.

"Alright, let's move."

But Diamond noticed something in the distance. "Damien, look out!" But it was too late. Dante held Damien down with a lightning harness that he couldn't break free from.

"You didn't really think we were done here, did you?" Dante taunted as he walked toward them. He knocked Nadia and Damien out and dragged her away as he released the harness on Damien. He quickly drew his attention to Diamond and grabbed her with the lightning harness and knocked her out.

By the time Damien woke up, he heard faint screams in the distance. "Damien! Damien!" they cried out. He looked up and saw both Diamond and Nadia tied to a chair sitting near the edge of the building. Damien's mind and heart began to race as he came to grips with the situation he was facing.

Dante stood in between the women clapping as Damien approached slowly. "There comes a time in every hero's journey where he's forced to make a choice, Damien. And no matter how difficult that choice may be, it has to be made. The quintessential impossible decision... This is that time for you. It's time to make a choice... a choice of which life to save. Will it be your fearless leader who led this army of yours to my front door or will it be your precious love?"

At that moment, Damien thought back to what Cyris had told him: "I guarantee you, if that psychopath out there gets the chance, he will use her against you. And nine times out of ten, you'll have to make a choice that you don't want to make: her life or the mission?"

Before Damien could have a moment to think, Dante pushed both of them off of the one-hundred-and-ten-story building. They both fell at intense speeds as Dante stood laughing in a most sinister manner. Without hesitation, Damien leaped off of the side of the building after them. He flew down as fast as he could to Nadia and took hold of her. She screamed in terror as she feared that they wouldn't survive the free fall. But just as it seemed to be the end, Damien released the ropes off of her and embraced her as they made their descent downward.

Once they reached the bottom and landed safely, Damien sat Nadia down and kissed her. "Go to Christian. Hurry!" he said as he propelled himself back up the side of the building to get Diamond.

As he went up, the wind and rain hit his face, but that didn't affect him as he made his ascent up the side of the building. As far as he was concerned, no one else was dying if he had anything to do with it.

When he finally got to Diamond, he had a difficult time untying her. Diamond started to get frustrated and began to tear up. "Damien, just go. Stop Dante, please," she pleaded. "Just leave me. It's alright."

But Damien kept trying. Losing another friend simply wasn't an option. He, then, began to harness the fire from the building into his hand and used it to burn the ropes from her wrists. Once freed, Damien dropped back down to the ground and ran over to Christian.

"Chris, I need you to get the wormhole device started up." Damien, then, looked over to Diamond. "Get the soldiers out of the way! This ends now!"

As he walked back toward the building, his eyes began to glow. He opened his hand and looked down at it and saw that he was forming a ball of strong electricity. Damien eventually was surrounded by an aura of electricity, pure power coming from within. As he walked, it overloaded all equipment that he walked past. All of the soldiers hid behind whatever they could to find safety.

Once he reached the building, Damien let out a scream as his aura became stronger. Then, something amazing happened. His entire body became engulfed in flames. The power surrounding him and flowing through him had everyone in awe as his power continued to increase.

Damien looked back. "Everyone get clear. I'm bringing the fight to the ground."

With that, he took off for the top of the building to face Dante once more as everyone looked on in anticipation of what was coming next.

CHAPTER 22

Everyone stood in awe around the building. Everything seemed and felt surreal, and they couldn't understand the extent of what was happening. Large, nightmarish creatures had become an everyday norm for two and a half years. Wormholes and explosive battles between two men opened up their eyes to tons of possibilities in the world. They had never seen anything of that magnitude before. The arrival of Dante showed them that anything is possible. But after seeing all that Damien was capable of, and how he could hold his own against such a threat, they started to believe in the incredible.

On the inside, Damien could feel his power growing stronger, more rabid, like a caged animal waiting to be released. It frightened him more than anything, though, to know that he held the ability to destroy everything in his path. But, too, it humbled him. It gave him a sense of purpose. He now understood why he survived the Event: so that he could be the one to save the world and the entire human race from annihilation.

Dante stood at his wormhole device reprogramming it so he could continue his mission to merge the dimensions. Just as he started the device back up and opened the portal over the city again, Damien grabbed him by the shoulder, turned him around, and punched him in the face.

The glow in Damien's eyes grew stronger as his rage took over. "I could kill you!" he shouted as they continued to fight.

Dante just laughed as they traded blow after blow in an unrelenting brawl. The fierce battle shook the foundation of what was left of the rooftop. Then, Dante decided to take the fight to new heights – literally...

As Dante started to raise himself into the air, Damien looked up at him with great anger, and then, the unexpected happened: a rush of static electricity flowed through his body and propelled him into the air and the fight continued.

Dante grappled with Damien and head-butted him before releasing a barrage of punches and energy attacks. He found tremendous joy in his fight with Damien. It was the challenge to his power that he had always looked for. It was a game to Dante, and he reveled in the fury of the battle. As he started toying with him, he grabbed Damien and flew him closer and closer to the wormhole above the tower.

Back on the ground, all they could do was watch the fight and wait for the outcome. All the soldiers cheered loudly for Damien to win. Christian sat on the back of the truck with the wormhole device waiting for them to come down while Diamond comforted Nadia.

"Do you think he can do it, Diamond?" Nadia asked.

Diamond just looked at the fight above. "I don't know," she said in a quiet tone. "I really don't know... But if anyone can pull this off, it's Damien. He's given hope to not only myself but everyone here watching and waiting. He's made us all believe in the impossible. He's given us hope – a light in the darkness. I don't think he realizes it, but he's fighting for the world right now. Not just Chicago. So, no matter what happens here, Damien is a hero, and I'm proud to have fought beside him."

Diamond's words were able to relax Nadia to the point she was no longer worried. She understood that Damien would do everything in his power to stop Dante. As she stood watching, she began to feel sick to her stomach to the point she ran to a nearby trash can and vomited.

Right away, Diamond ran to her side. "What's wrong? Are you alright?"

"Yeah, I'm fine," Nadia replied. "It's just a little stomach bug. I'll be alright."

Diamond didn't press the issue with Nadia, but she knew that something was off. Nadia rarely got sick and this was out of the ordinary. As soon as they walked back over to the crowd, Christian hopped off the back of the truck. "Alright, the machine is ready to go. We just need them to come back down."

Damien, seeing that they were ready, turned the fight around in an instant. "It's time to put an end to this," Damien stated calmly.

Just as the dimensions were about to collide, Damien drove Dante down from the edge of the wormhole into his machine and it exploded almost immediately causing a massive explosion, but half of the goal was finished. And that was to close Dante's portal above the city.

Damien got up from the wreckage and looked down at Dante who lay there barely clinging to life after the fall. "You don't deserve mercy..." He, then, picked Dante up with one hand and held him high into the sky. Using the other hand, Damien charged an energy blast of fire and electricity and shot Dante in the stomach, severely injuring him. "But I want you to remember this moment for the rest of your natural life. And the next time you try to come here or even think that you want to try to come here, I need you to think about this moment long and hard and remember the face of the man that took you down and truly understand that, if there is a next time, I won't be so merciful."

Dante, barely hanging on to life, agreed just as Damien knocked him out.

The thunderstorm started to subside as Damien stood contemplating what the future had in store. Would he stay and help the Pack rebuild? Would he leave for a while so that he could test the limits of his powers? What he knew was that the future, now, felt more promising for a change now that Dante had finally been defeated.

The rainfall helped to diminish the fire around them on the rooftop. Their battle left enormous amounts of damage in their wake. Ready to meet the others, Damien grabbed Dante's body and levitated above the carnage. He, then, flew around and searched the area for Cyris' body.

Finding him proved to be a difficult task, though. He used energy blasts to destroy most of the rubble to make it easier to navigate through. Just when he thought that he should give up, he found Cyris' body, lifted him with his free arm, threw him over his shoulder, and flew down to the ground.

As he landed, Damien was greeted with thunderous applause from all of the soldiers. Christian, Nadia, and Diamond ran to Damien to greet him. Everyone was beyond overjoyed at the fact that the war was finally over. Damien threw Dante to the ground and handed Cyris' body over to Diamond and the soldiers. Nadia embraced Damien tightly as everyone continued to cheer. It was a real cause for celebration as they could finally see peace in view.

Damien, then, raised his hand high in the air to request their silence. "Today is a cause for celebration. We've finally won this war. Dante has been defeated. But let's not forget those that sacrificed everything for us to get here. We've come a long way. Now, it's time for us to rebuild our lives. It's time we took back what's ours!"

Christian reached into his pocket and pulled out the remote to his wormhole device. "You guys ready to do this?" he asked.

Damien nodded in agreement. He, then, turned and looked at Nadia and kissed her. "What do you say we go find a beach and just get away for a while?"

Nadia smiled. "I'd love that... a lot," she said. "Look, there's something that I need to tell you. I'm pretty excited but absolutely terrified at the same time."

"Sure, what's up?" Damien asked.

Just as Nadia was about to speak...

"You fools. Do you really believe that because Damien beat me that this is all over?"

They all turned to face Dante as he stood up. "Do you think that this all started with me? No, no, no."

"Stay down, Dante," Damien told him boldly. "It's over. Don't you get it? You're finished."

"No, Damien. I'm just the beginning. And by not allowing me to complete my mission, you have just effectively doomed this entire planet along with every other known realm."

"What are saying, Dante?" Christian demanded.

"Do you need me to spell it out for you? Your world is now a target of the most powerful monstrosity known to the universe. My former master. And he's coming. There isn't anything or anyone here to stop him. Damien won't be enough."

"I beat you, Dante," Damien boasted. "I'm sure I can face whatever is coming."

Dante chuckled in pain as he held his side. "You know, son, you amuse me. So naive. Believe me, you will need every ounce of strength you can muster up to get the job done. This was my goal in coming here, Damien. To this dimension and this time, it was all to get you ready. I knew what you were capable of before you did."

"How?" Damien asked. "How could you?"

Dante reached up and removed his hood. He unlatched his mask from the sides and removed it before he held his head up and revealed his face. A quarter of his face was badly burned with heavy scar tissue. The grey stubble on his face shined in the headlights of the trucks.

No one could believe what they were seeing. Especially Damien, Nadia, Christian, and Diamond. The shock froze them where they were.

"How is it possible?" Christian asked.

"Your eyes aren't deceiving you," Dante said.

"You're me," Damien said hesitantly. "But you're older..."

"About twenty-four years older to be exact," Dante said. "I come from a dimension and future much different from this reality. A reality where everything is in ruins and humanity is nearly extinct."

"But you just tried to destroy all of us," Damien argued. "You destroyed families and ruined this Earth."

"Don't you get it? I didn't have another way. I needed you to awaken. I knew that I wouldn't be able to stop him or the destruction he would bring. I thought that maybe you would join me, and help me complete my mission — my life's work. It had to be you, Damien. It still does. But know this... This journey will tear you apart. Every fiber of your being will be tested in ways you never thought possible. You need to let go of all of this and be free from attachments because anyone close to you will be a distraction and a target. They will never be safe, they will never be truly free, and they will only hold you back."

Without hesitation, Damien stated. "I'll never do that, Dante. They're my family and family sticks together no matter what. I told you before that I sympathized with you and what happened with your family. I really do. But my family is my strength, not my weakness."

Dante grew hot with anger. Christian noticed the situation was about to get tense, so he started up the wormhole device right away directly behind Dante. He motioned for everyone to move back.

Dante started to charge up an energy blast. "If you won't do it, Damien, then I'll do it for you!"

He, then, fired the blast toward Nadia. She stood frozen as the blast came toward her. Damien quickly jumped in front of the blast and deflected it. In a last-ditch effort to rid everyone of Dante, Damien rushed toward him and tackled him into the wormhole. But the unexpected happened: Damien went through with him. And just as he fell through, Damien shot a blast of his own from the wormhole to the device, destroying it instantly and closing the portal behind him.

"NO!" Nadia cried out as she fell to her knees. She gripped Diamond's leg as she burst into tears. "Open the portal, Chris! Bring him back!" she shouted.

"I can't," Christian said. "He fried the system. It's toast."

Nadia stayed frozen, still clutching onto Diamond's leg. "How could he leave, Diamond? How could he leave us?"

Diamond knelt to embrace Nadia and give her comfort. "We'll find him. He'll come back to us. I promise."

Nadia wiped the tears from her eyes and looked up at Diamond. "No, you don't understand, Diamond. I'm pregnant. He doesn't know."

Christian and Diamond both held Nadia close offering her a measure of solace. But the fact remained that not only did they lose a mentor and leader in Cyris, but also, a friend, a brother, a lover, and a protector in Damien.

CHapter 23

The next few days proved difficult for Nadia. She had gone over those last moments in her head repeatedly trying to figure out if there was something that she could've done differently to ensure that he stayed. Despite her best efforts, she couldn't cope with the fact that Damien was gone. Adding to her fear was the prospect of being a mother and possibly raising her child without its father. It was the most terrifying feeling that she felt in years.

She spent most of her time sitting in the hospital bed where she first saw Damien wishing over and over that he would come back. Nadia replayed the moment of him flying into the portal repeatedly wishing things had panned out a lot differently. But the reality was that he was gone, and no one knew for certain when or if he was ever coming back.

The day of the memorial service for Cyris was especially difficult for Diamond. She replayed in her head time and again the moments leading up to his death wondering if she could've saved him, or if she could've sacrificed herself instead. She was heartbroken, having lost so much already. And this was no different. As she sat in her office making final arrangements, Christian walked in and sat down.

"How are you holding up?" he asked.

"Considering that we're burying the man that has been a father to me for the past two years, I guess I'm doing alright. Aside from the crying, puffy eyes, and sleepless nights, I guess I'm doing the best I can. It's just hard to accept the fact that he's gone. He was such a big part of, not only my life but everyone here. It's a huge loss for us all. I just wish that he knew what he meant to me as a mentor and father figure."

"Yeah, I understand all that," Christian stated. "I'm sure he knew. It's tough for us all. Too many losses to count. Not just Cyris, but Damien, too. Not to mention everyone else that we lost over the years."

"I know, right? Speaking of which, have you talked to Nadia lately?"

Christian said with a sigh, "I have here and there. She's taking Damien being gone pretty hard. As much as I try to stay positive, it's hard trying to assure her that he'll be back when I don't even know it myself. It's crazy, you know? They fell in love with each other at the same time he was going through his struggles with his 'awakening' and then she got pregnant – which was a surprise to all of us. It's like, now what? What does she do?"

"I know what you mean," Diamond acknowledged. "We're both gonna have to be there for her. What about you? You haven't really said much about it."

"I know. I'm OK, I guess. I miss my brother. That's for sure. It's different not having him around to look after me. Don't get me wrong, though. I get why he did what he did. It makes my admiration and respect for him that much greater. In the end, I guess, no one won. We lost too much to get where we are now.

Not only have we lost our actual families, but now our family here is fractured. And honestly, I don't think it'll ever be whole again. Yeah, Damien might come back, and their family is expanding. But without Cyris, it just feels like there's a gap there that can't be filled again."

"I know what you mean. It kind of makes you think, though, about what's next."

"Yeah, definitely. Have you thought about what I said to you before?"

"Yeah," she said as she sat back in her chair. "Do you think we can make it work? Don't get me wrong. I would love to, but..."

Christian stood up and walked around the desk to Diamond and took hold of her hand and kissed it. "We have the whole future ahead of us to figure it out. We can do this," Christian said. He kissed her and walked out of the room as Diamond smiled from ear to ear.

Meanwhile, Nadia kept a constant vigil in Damien's room at the clinic. For her, that room held some of the fondest memories that she had experienced in two years. The moment she laid eyes on Damien was the moment she felt complete, whole even. Now, without him there to talk to her, hold her, comfort her, and love her, she didn't know where to turn or what to do.

The prospect of being a single mother weighed on her mind as well. What would the child be like without its father around? Would she be a good mother? Would Damien be back to help pick up the pieces and make their family whole again? She didn't know, and it bothered her immensely. But she knew that she had to keep pushing forward, not only for her but her unborn child. She needed to keep looking towards the future regardless of if Damien returned or not.

Nadia eventually found herself in Damien's room, holding onto memories of the two of them. She soon found her way to the bed. As she lay down, she clutched the pillow tightly hoping to catch his scent.

"I miss you so much right now," she began. "We haven't been together long, but it feels like a lifetime. Now, I'm without you and I don't know what to do. You came into my life like a storm, and just as suddenly, you're gone. I don't know where you are, or if you're even alive. I just hope that you come back to me... to us." Just as she finished speaking, she cried herself to sleep.

Later that day, in the auditorium, everyone in the complex gathered for the memorial service of Cyris. On the stage, to the right of the podium was Cyris' casket with a picture of him standing on one side. On the other side stood a picture of Damien.

The occasion was bittersweet, indeed. It was a celebration of life, love, and the victory they had all achieved together. And there was much reason to celebrate. Dante and his Night-stalkers were gone, and the world was now free. But that freedom came with a heavy cost. On the other hand, it was an occasion that also called for mourning because of the loss of their comrades. Two of their finest soldiers were gone. And no amount of celebration could bring them back.

As Diamond approached the podium, the crowd greeted her with thunderous applause. The people cheered so loudly that the entire complex began to shake. She stood smiling before the people while holding back her tears. She was emotional and began to feel overwhelmed. "Diamond! Diamond!" they shouted repeatedly. The chants of her name got louder and louder with each passing second. Through the applause and internal pain and heartache, Diamond pulled herself together and then raised her hand for silence. As they quieted down, Diamond began to speak.

"I am pleased to inform all of you that this two-year-long war is finally over!" The crowd cheered loudly again but she quickly regained their attention. "We've fought long and hard for this moment. We have a chance to return to the surface. We have the chance to rebuild our homes and raise our children in a world where we don't need to live in fear. We finally have the chance to live again. Over the next few weeks, my team, and I will be working on plans to make the migration back to the surface. With all of that being said, let us never forget the sacrifices of our friends, Cyris and Damien, because, without them, none of this would even be possible."

She continued: "For those of you that got to know Cyris over the past two years, you'll recall how loving and how caring and generous he was. You may have sat down and talked with him about his military days, or what the world was like before The Event. You may have gotten advice from him or vice versa. You see, Cyris never came across as unloving or unwilling. He was always ready to lend a hand to someone in need and he didn't hesitate. To know him was to love him. And for that, we should all be thankful for having someone like that in our midst. But he's gone now after making the ultimate sacrifice. One that he made without hesitation or pause. He was a soldier until the very end. So, as we lay him to rest today, try very hard to remember and observe what a wonderful person that James Collins was."

"Now, what could I say of Damien? I watched him over the past few months grow into a remarkable young man. His bravery and his quest for justice knew absolutely no bounds. Many of you don't know or may not be aware, but Damien lost everything in The Event. He lost his home, his parents, and his sister. He endured so much. And that is what was remarkable about him. He never said 'quit.' He kept moving no matter what. No matter how badly the odds were stacked against him, he kept fighting. He fought not just for himself, but for the freedom of the entire world. And for that, we should all be grateful. Now, where he is now, none of us know. But we will do whatever it takes to find him and bring him home for good. That's a promise."

"For now, we rebuild. We prepare to take back our world and reshape the future. This is what they had in mind when they gave of themselves. They would want us to make a better world – a better world than we had before The Event. And we'll make sure that we carry that out to the fullest of our abilities!"

The crowd went crazy. They were all finally free to forge their destinies and make their marks on the world. Now was the time to live and be fruitful.

That evening, Nadia sat on the rooftop and looked out over the city. The quiet was a sound that hadn't happened in a long time. It was refreshing to her to see a calm night and enjoy the fresh air.

Christian and Diamond soon joined her.

"It's nice, isn't it?" Nadia asked.

"To hear nothing but silence," Christian said. "Absolutely. I just hope it lasts."

"Why do you say that?" Diamond inquired. "Dante is gone and all of his Night-stalkers are dead."

Nadia stated, "He's talking about what Dante said before they went through the portal. Yeah, I don't think that the quiet will last. I mean, I'll enjoy it while we have it, but I won't be caught unprepared. Not this time. I'm gonna be ready."

"If that's the case," Diamond said, "then we need an advantage. Let's face it. None of us are like Damien and I don't think there will be another."

"So, we find him," Christian suggested. "I'm not giving up on him. And when it comes down to it, he needs us just as much as we need him. We're all family now, right? Family sticks together."

"I'd be lying to you if I said that I wasn't scared," Nadia stated. "I'm literally shaking right now. My palms are so sweaty. I'm gonna be a mother in eight more months. And now the father of my baby is missing... What am I going to do?"

Diamond gave Nadia a big hug to comfort her. "We're gonna help you. You won't be alone. You're never alone. And besides, you'll be a great mother. You'll raise your baby to value life and cherish the smaller things in life - things that we may have forgotten over time. But don't doubt yourself. And when Damien comes back, he'll appreciate you even more for it."

Everyone hugged each other for a while and then looked out over the city. Peace had finally come back to Chicago and the rest of the world. All the pain and hurt over the past two years were now erased and everyone could now get on with their lives and start to rebuild.

As Nadia looked up to the stars, she said a silent prayer and a sense of serenity came over her. Quietly, to herself, she said, "I love you, Damien," and they all went back inside to rest peacefully through the night.

Tomorrow, The Future Begins...

EPILOGUE

T hree years later in an alternate universe and time...

The skies over Chicago gradually dimmed over the daytime sky. Strong winds howled through the tall buildings downtown. It was a quiet morning not unlike usual. Soldiers were scattered about at every intersection patrolling the streets. The few citizens that remained hid away in whatever abandoned storefront or dark corner that they could find.

The city had been placed under martial law over the last three years by its ruthless leader. The people that were left in this wasteland of a city weren't free to live the way that they wanted to and had no control over their own lives. There was no contact with the outside world because there wasn't a world to contact. Chicago was the last remaining metropolis of the world.

On this particular day, constant earthquakes rocked the city. No one knew what to think of the situation. But meanwhile, in one of the city's skyscrapers...

"Sir," the scientist said. "Everything is almost set to go. Just a few more adjustments and we'll be ready for transport."

In a dark room, a young woman was laying on an operating table. Her open scalp revealed a tiny microchip resting on her exposed brain. Waiting in the shadows, a tall figure stood in the corner watching over the procedure.

"Are you sure that this will work the way that I want it to?" he inquired. "I don't want there to be any mistakes. There's no room for error."

"Yes, my Lord," the scientist answered nervously. "Once she arrives, after about forty-eight hours, the programming will kick in and she'll be active."

"Good," the leader said as he exited the room.

He walked down the hallway to the elevator and stood motionless as he gazed out the window overlooking the city. He reveled in the destruction and chaos. And at the same time, he appreciated the silence that his rule brought over the city.

Once the elevator arrived, he got on it and rode it to the top floor. As he got off, his wife greeted him right away.

"My beloved, are you alright?" she asked.

"Yes, I'm fine. It's almost time. She will depart within the next two hours. My men are making the final preparations now."

"Are you sure that this is what you want to do?" she asked.

He took her hand and led her to their dinner table. As he sat her down, he slowly kissed her hand and then sat across from her.

"I've never been more sure of anything in my life," the leader assured her, "except the day that I decided to make you my bride."

She sighed. "I don't want to lose her. We never had a chance to have a daughter, and our son is gone..."

In a rage, he threw the cup next to him across the room. "Our son made his choice! Now, where is he? Huh? Where is he?! He's dead now. His mistakes, his greed, his... so-called moral compass and sudden change of heart... - all of it was his undoing."

"Undoing?" she interrupted. "You had our son killed! Your anger is what pushed him away. Your anger is what drove him to the one who is now our master. We don't live free anymore. And now you've made the world share in this mess. Take responsibility for your hand in his fate!"

Enraged, he rose from the table, stormed over to his wife, and furiously hit her with the back of his hand knocking her to the floor.

"Don't you dare speak to me in that manner!" He then turned over the dinner table violently. "If it wasn't for our son, we wouldn't be where we are now! He set this in motion the moment he left us. And now, I'm going to do what he would've never thought to do and there isn't any stopping it. You have the audacity to speak to me about responsibility?! Where were you, his mother, when he was..."

"Don't you dare put this on me!" she rebutted. "You wanted him gone the second you found out what he was." She stood up and wiped the blood from her mouth. "And now look at you. You're the same as him. And now you want to avenge him? Start by killing yourself because it was your orders, your will, and your soldiers that did the job. His blood is on your hands!"

He took a long pause. "That's true. His blood is on my hands. But the ones who turned him, they'll pay their price as well. Nothing else matters; Not this world, any of the people in it, or even what Lord Draco has to say. I don't care anymore."

With that, he stormed out of their suite and went back downstairs to the lab where they were holding the young woman.

Meanwhile, the leader's wife took the time to clean up the mess that her husband had made. After doing that she stood at the window staring out into the empty city streets. She questioned if supporting his quest for vengeance was the right thing to do. Who else would needlessly suffer because of the tirades of a madman?

As she looked to the sky, she said to herself, "What should I do? Could this be the fall of our world? Is this how it ends?"

Soon after, the leader arrived at the laboratory in an extremely bad mood.

"Is she ready?!" he demanded.

His workers cowered in fear of displeasing him. The lead scientist spoke: "Not quite, sir. There's a problem with the interface. The fault in the chip could potentially be exposed."

His temper grew hotter by the second. Infuriated, he slammed his fist on the table next to him. "Never mind the interface. Can she make the trip and be intact as she is? That's all I need to know right now."

Nervously, the scientist answered, "Yes, my lord. She can make the trip. But there's an eighty-five percent chance that you may lose your control over her. Do you want to take that kind of risk, sir?"

"It doesn't matter. Nothing matters anymore. Prep her for the transport."

Right away, the scientist began stitching up the woman's scalp. Once that was finished, he and his assistants placed her in a wheelchair and pushed her out of the room while she was still unconscious. As they made their way down the hall towards the elevator, another earthquake shook the city. As the leader tried to catch his balance, he grabbed onto the woman's arm.

"It's cold," he said. "Why is she so cold? It's warm in here."

"It's her abilities, sir. They're beginning to manifest."

A large smile hit the leader's face. "Ah, this is even better than I planned. It's her awakening. The quakes... Is this her, too?"

"We don't know," the scientist replied. "I suppose it's possible. It isn't like we haven't seen one person possess multiple abilities."

"Interesting..."

Once the quake subsided, they all got on the elevator and rode it down to the basement. Immediately, they went to the transport machine where the engineer was preparing the machine.

"My lord," the engineer started. "Final preparations are set. She'll arrive exactly in this spot on the other Earth. There are soldiers already there marching around the city. But once she arrives, she's on her own. Her programming will take hold soon after."

"Good. Send her through."

With that, the assistants to the scientist lifted the woman and pushed her through the open wormhole. The leader stood watching with a smile on his face as his plan was now set in motion and no one was there to stop him. And just as he exited the room laughing to himself, the engineer closed the wormhole and shut down the machine all while hearing the leader walk down the corridor with a maniacal laugh knowing the carnage that he just unleashed.

www.ingramcontent.com/pod-product-compliance
Lightning Source LLC
Chambersburg PA
CBHW070314190726

48291CB00013B/1294